D1037618

STICK
PICK

STICK PICK

STEVEN SANDOR

James Lorimer & Company Ltd., Publishers
Toronto

Copyright © 2017 by Steven Sandor
Published in Canada in 2017.

All rights reserved. No part of this book may be reproduced or transmitted in
any form or by any means, electronic or mechanical, including photocopying,
or by any information storage or retrieval system, without permission in writing
from the publisher.

James Lorimer & Company Ltd., Publishers acknowledges the support of
the Ontario Arts Council (OAC), an agency of the Government of Ontario,
which in 2015-16 funded 1,676 individual artists and 1,125 organizations in
209 communities across Ontario for a total of $50.5 million. We acknowledge
the support of the Canada Council for the Arts, which last year invested $153
million to bring the arts to Canadians throughout the country. This project
has been made possible in part by the Government of Canada and with the
support of the Ontario Media Development Corporation.

Cover design: Shabnam Safari
Cover image: Connor Mah, Flickr

Library and Archives Canada Cataloguing in Publication

Sandor, Steven, 1971-, author
    Stick pick / Steven Sandor.

(Sports stories)
Issued in print and electronic formats.
ISBN 978-1-4594-1219-4 (softcover).--ISBN 978-1-4594-1221-7 (EPUB)

    I. Title.

PS8637.A547S75 2017   jC813'.6   C2017-903299-2
                                               C2017-903300-X

Published by: Distributed in Canada by: Distributed in the US by:
James Lorimer &   Formac Lorimer Books   Lerner Publisher Services
Company Ltd., Publishers   5502 Atlantic Street   1251 Washington Ave. N.
117 Peter Street, Suite 304   Halifax, NS, Canada   Minneapolis, MN, USA
Toronto, ON, Canada   B3H 1G4   55401
M5V 0M3   www.lernerbooks.com
www.lorimer.ca

Manufactured by Marquis in Montmagny, Quebec, Canada in July 2017.
Job #142280

*Dedicated to all of you who have been told
you'll never be able to do something,
but went ahead and did it anyway.*

Contents

1 THE OVERTIME WINNER

Janine streaks down the ice. Her skates make a *shush-shush* sound as she skates across the blue line. A defender tries to cut her off. Janine passes the puck to her best friend, Rowena Khan, who is rushing down the left wing.

Excuse me, Miss? Can you hear me? Miss? She's not responsive.

Janine doesn't stop skating. She goes toward the net. She keeps her stick on the ice. She feels in her gut that Rowena is going to send her a return pass.

We have to cut her free. She's pinned. Everyone, clear!

Rowena stops at the half-boards. She fires a low, crisp pass toward the crease. Her skates flash as she stops in front of the net. She reaches her stick out and feels the puck hit the blade.

We have her free! Now, easy, easy . . . get her onto the stretcher. Keep that spine straight! The helicopter is three minutes away.

With a quick flick of the wrists, Janine whips her

stick forward. The puck rockets into the top corner of the net and the red goal light comes on. Janine raises her stick in the air. Then she is knocked to the ice, not by an opponent, but by her teammates. They pile on her in celebration.

Miss, can you hear us? Can you? We're going to be airlifting you to University Hospital in Edmonton. I've got a pulse of 110. She's breathing, but she's not responsive.

Janine and her teammates line up on their blue line. The tournament convener shakes Coach Sibierski's hand. Next, it's Janine's turn.

"Nice winning goal, Captain," the convener says. He places a shiny gold medal around Janine's neck. And then he says at the top of his lungs, "Our tournament champions, the Edmonton Ice Devils!"

The Ice Devils bang their sticks on the ice.

We have to get her to the OR. Are we prepped? Yes, the driver was taken to emergency. He's conscious. I don't have the status on the other passenger. I think it was her mother. Keep the father informed of our progress.

Janine and her teammates cheer loudly in their dressing room. The trophy stands in the middle of the room. Crossed golden hockey sticks sit atop a silver globe. Janine picks up the trophy and kisses it.

There's severe damage below the T6 vertebra. I don't know how much we can do. Let's clean up the wound. We'll see how much movement she has once we get her to recovery. Let's hope for the best.

The Overtime Winner

Janine gets into the back seat of the SUV. She waves goodbye to her teammates in the parking lot.

Her dad pulls out of the Westlock Arena's parking lot. They drive back to Edmonton, south on Highway 44.

"What a game!" Janine's dad says. "I got that entire scoring play on my phone! Maybe I'll write an article about it for tomorrow's Sports section."

Her mom looks back at Janine from the front seat. "Wow. I mean, wow. Overtime winner! I was so, so nervous."

"That was more exciting than any pro game I've ever covered," says Janine's dad.

"Okay, Dad," Janine's eyes roll.

Headlights appear ahead of them and then disappear. Cars zip by on the two-lane highway. And, then, two sets of headlights loom in front of them. One is off in the other lane, and one is directly in the path of their SUV.

Mr. and Mrs. Burnett? Your daughter is waking up. Are you okay? We're calling for Dr. Ali right now.

★ ★ ★

Janine's eyes fluttered open. She heard beeping noises from the machine next to her bed. On the screen was a 79 next to a flashing heart symbol. Underneath, there was a display that read Oxygen: 94%. It changed to 95. Then back to 94.

Stick Pick

There were tubes coming out of Janine's right arm, which was wrapped in white tape. Stitches went from her left elbow almost down to her wrist. Her body felt tingly, as if her legs and arms had been asleep.

A nurse in a green gown stood next to the bed. Janine looked toward the window and saw her dad sitting in a chair. His head was bandaged. His eyes were red and swollen. Next to him was her mom. She sat in a wheelchair. Bandages covered almost half of her face. Tubes ran from an IV drip into her arm.

"Dad? Mom?" Janine tried to say. But it came out as a hoarse whisper. All she could get out was a barely audible, "*aaah, ommm.*"

Mr. Burnett pushed himself out of his chair with great effort. He was in a gown and had a hospital ID bracelet on his wrist. He shuffled toward Janine until he was close enough to take her left hand.

"I am so, so sorry," he said.

Janine's mom was silent. The one eye that Janine could see was yellow.

"Mom is sedated," her dad said. "She's in a lot of pain. But we thought it was important for her to be here with you."

"Pain?" Janine said. "Is she going to be okay?"

"The doctors say she'll be fine." Janine could tell by her dad's face that he wasn't telling her the truth. "It will be a long road back, though."

A doctor in a white coat walked into the room.

"Miss Burnett? Awake? How are you feeling?"

"Excuse me?" Janine said. "I mean, we were just driving home a minute ago, from the game."

The doctor gave Janine's parents a long, serious look. Then, he whispered something into the nurse's ear.

"Janine," her dad said. "We were in an accident. A week ago."

A week? Janine thought. *I just got into the car a few minutes ago! We just won the tournament!*

The doctor lifted the sheet covering Janine's legs. He got a small silver instrument out of his pocket. At the end of a long handle was a wheel covered in small picks. He rolled the picked wheel against her right leg, then her left leg.

"Do you feel anything?"

"No, just a tingling in my legs."

The doctor spoke quickly to the nurse. Janine heard "spine," "vertebra," "compression" and "damage."

She looked back toward her dad. His face was covered by his right hand. Tears streamed through his fingers.

"Dad? What's wrong? Why am I here?"

2 REHAB

Janine wriggled. It was a struggle to get out of her bed and settle into her wheelchair. She looked at the calendar on the bedside dresser that showed how long she'd been in the hospital. It had a month's worth of Xs drawn through the boxes. On the other side, another month's worth of Xs.

As soon as Janine began moving, waves of nausea returned. The doctors had told her that was normal for anyone who had suffered a severe spinal injury. They said it would go away after a couple of months.

It's been a couple of months now, right? she thought.

She had no feeling in her legs. So, when she moved, her brain responded with *hey, why do our eyes tell me we're moving when our legs aren't telling me anything?* The response to the mixed messages was the sick feeling. It was like feeling carsick when she read a comic book in the back seat of a moving car.

Janine wheeled herself to the common room. It was where patients at the Glenrose Rehabilitation Hospital ate, met with friends and played games.

Janine saw Rowena walk into the common area and sit at a table near the corner. Janine rolled herself toward her best friend.

"Hi," Rowena said. She pushed a pink envelope and a small, gift-wrapped box across the table.

"I told you this wasn't a good idea," said Janine. She pushed the envelope and box away. She didn't make eye contact with Rowena.

"Why? It's been a few weeks. I missed you. I wanted to see you earlier. But you kept saying no, no, no . . ."

"And I'll keep saying no!" Janine snapped. "I don't need my friends throwing me a pity party. Just give me the chance to get better. And then we can hang out like old times."

"Better?" Rowena asked. Her eyebrows curled up. "So, what does that, um . . . mean? I thought you couldn't get better. Okay, I mean, how do I say this . . . ?"

"That's just it," Janine said. "I knew you'd come here and not know how to talk to me."

"I'm trying, Janine."

Janine rolled slightly back, then forward again, not looking up. "What I'm saying is that when I get better we'll all be back to normal. There's no need for you to be here right now. I don't want you to think of me sitting here in the hospital."

"So, you can get better?" Rowena almost smiled

for half a second. "Is that what the doctors say?"

"No, the doctors, so far . . . well, they say this is permanent. But my parents are going to ask for more opinions. I'm not giving up hope. The accident wasn't all that long ago, was it? Maybe I can heal. Maybe there's a doctor out there who can help me so I can walk and skate again."

"I guess, sure. Maybe?" Rowena said quietly.

Janine brought her fist down on the table. "What I'm sure of is that you're not helping. At all."

Rowena rose from her chair. "Look, I can tell you're not in the mood to talk. But, like it or not, I'm going to come here again. And again. I've been your best friend since kindergarten. No accident is going to change that."

As Rowena walked away, Janine looked down at her smartphone. There was a message on the home screen.

Dad: Got some good news! Talk to you later.

Good news, thought Janine. *Like, when does that ever happen? The nerve of Rowena. She came here even though I asked her not to.*

Janine looked around the common area. There were other patients in wheelchairs. They were young, old, girls, boys, men, women. In the corner was Bob. She heard he'd lost a leg in an accident on a worksite in Fort McMurray. There was Steve, who walked with canes.

Rehab

Despite feeling sick, Janine thought about wheeling into the kitchen to get something to eat. It was like she was really hungry, but wanted to throw up at the same time. She decided to wheel back to her room.

On the desk next to Janine's bed was a tablet. She turned it on and opened the "Patient Diary" file.

There were more than fifty entries. As she had drifted in and out of awareness after the accident, nurses had made reports. Janine and her parents were able to look back and see how she recovered. There were medical reports. There were bits about "broken vertebrae" and "permanent damage" and "quality of life."

Now, Janine was making entries as well.

PATIENT DIARY:

Today, my best friend Rowena came to visit, even though I told her not to. She brought me a stupid gift. In the box is a championship medal from the team. Like I'd want that. There are two kinds of visits:

A visit from someone filled with bits where no one knows what to say. Super uncomfortable! (Rowena's visit)

The tragedy visit. Like when Grandma June wouldn't stop crying and crying and crying. She talked about things like "God's plan" and how I'd always need someone to look after me. Really good for the self-esteem!

Only dad tries to be normal. But I can tell by the crappy
beard and his clothes all looking too big that he's
pretty messed up about me and mom. But he texted
me that he has good news. So, there's that.

Janine was in her bed, reading, when her dad
walked in.

"Hey, there, Champ," he smiled. "What's that?"

"Some stupid book I have to write an essay about,"
she said.

"I thought you liked to read." He pulled a chair up
to the bed and sat down.

"I do," Janine rolled her eyes. "But not this stupid
book."

"And what makes it so stupid?" Her dad eyed the
cover. "That's a Canadian classic, you know."

"Oh, come on. I'm a hundred pages in and nothing
has happened."

"Then you won't mind putting it down."

Janine slid in the bookmark, closed the book and
tossed it onto the table next to the bed.

"Okay, here's the news." Her dad leaned forward, as
if he was about to tell her a secret. "First, your mother is
doing well. She walked more today than she has, well,
since the accident. She's got the cane and she still needs
to rest a bit. But the doctors say she's doing well. She
pushed herself."

"That's why she's not here?"

Rehab

"Yup," her dad nodded. "She's at home resting and, well, doing what she can to get the house ready."

"Ready?"

"I've been talking to Dr. Wells. And he's pleased with your progress. He wants to keep seeing you, but you don't need to be here 24-7. You can come home."

"Home?" Janine said. "But I'm not better yet."

"Well, the doctor says you're doing really well. You can get around fine. Your eating habits are improving. You're . . ."

"But that's not getting better, is it?" Janine snapped. "Dad, you make me so mad sometimes! Getting better is when I can roll out of my bed . . . wait, bad choice of words. Better is when I can walk to the bathroom! When I can walk to school!"

"Janine, Dr. Wells and Dr. Ali have talked to us about moving on. It is time for you to go back to school, not just do your schoolwork from a hospital bed."

"I'm not better, dad," said Janine. "Please don't make me go until I am."

3 COMING HOME

Janine's dad steered the minivan into the driveway. Janine looked out the window, bug-eyed.

"What have you done to the house?" she asked.

There used to be three steps that led from the driveway to the front door. Now, a ramp snaked its way onto the front lawn and up to the door.

"I don't believe it," Janine said. "First you pick me up in this grandpa van. I mean, I thought you'd get something better with the insurance money. And now, the house . . ."

"Wait until you get inside," her dad said. He walked around to the van's sliding side door. Once the door was open, a ramp lowered. Janine unlocked the anchor that secured her wheelchair to the floor of the van. Then she rolled down. She moved off the driveway and onto the walkway that led to her house, working her way up the incline. She felt her dad's hands on the wheelchair handles, so she put up her hand.

"Don't, Dad. I need to do this myself."

Coming Home

The door was new, with the handle placed lower than it had been. The doorway was wider.

"This should make it easier for you," her dad said.

"Seems to me you went to a lot of expense," Janine smiled. "Are we gonna keep the house like this when I get better? Everything is going to seem too wide or low. I'll have to crouch to open the door."

Her dad didn't reply. He just turned a key in the lock and opened the door.

Inside were more changes. The beat-up living room carpet was gone. Polished hardwood shone in its place.

"Dad, was the accident the thing that finally convinced you and mom to get rid of that brown carpet? I guess every cloud does have a silver lining."

"Hi, Janine," her mom's voice called from the dining room. Her mom sat at the table. A cane was placed across her lap. On the table were piles of papers and newspaper clippings and an open laptop.

Should I tell Mom how much older she looks, now? Janine wondered. *I mean, she had a few grey hairs on her head before the accident. But now she's got a full head of grey. Wow. I can see how much she looks like Grandma June, now.*

"We have a cake in the fridge." Janine's mom turned to look at her daughter. "Sorry, I lost track of the time! I've been busy writing letters to MPs and MLAs and the Crown Prosecutor."

"I think they all are pretty caught up on the case," said Janine. "I mean, we were front-page news for awhile. I could Google 'accident' and 'Edmonton' and we were, like, the top ten hits."

Janine's comeback didn't stop her mom. She started talking about the last thing her daughter wanted to hear — the accident. Janine tried to tune it out. She tried to think about any thing else. *What kind of cake is in the fridge? Chocolate? Does it have cherry filling?*

"He was on his cell phone," her mom said.

Janine tried to think of every player who was on Canada's 2012 Olympic gold medal team.

Her mom said, "we need better laws" and "victim-impact statement." Janine thought about how she'd rather have Dr. Ali dragging the picked wheel all over her legs.

Finally, her mom's voice stopped.

"Okay, great!" Janine said.

"Great? Great?!" her mom cried. "Janine Burnett, have you heard a word I've said?"

"Yeah, about the victim needing to have rights and laws against cell phones . . ."

"That victim is you! Now that you're home, you need to meet with the Crown Prosecutor. She's going to collect a victim-impact statement from you. You can read it in court. Or have it read for you."

"Okay," Janine's dad said, throwing up his hands. "I think we can give our daughter a bit of time, now.

She's got a lot to process."

"We're also going to need to talk about getting you to school, and your dad getting back to work." Janine's mom tapped her fingernails against the metal shaft of her cane. It was like she was trying to send a coded message.

"School? Work?" Janine asked. It was all coming so fast. How long had she been in the house? Five minutes?

"Look, Janine," her dad said as he sat at the table across from her mom. "I wasn't going to talk about this until after the cake. But your mom has been edgy. A reporter like me, well, sooner or later we will run out of money. I've exhausted all my leave days."

"And we're almost out of benefit money for this year," said her mom. "We spent almost all our savings renovating this house."

"Mom can't go back to work for a few more months. So, I have to get back on the beat," her dad said. He was doing his best to avoid eye contact with Janine. "And it also means going back to school, for you. I've been talking to the principal and our school trustee. They say they've made all the arrangements. Next Monday, you can go back. They'll have a special bus — I mean, a van — to pick you up and bring you home."

Janine felt dizzy. She couldn't go to school like this! Her friends would be there!

"You know what?" Janine said. "This is all my

fault. Everything. You didn't have to do this all for me! You should have just left me in the hospital!"

And, for the first time since the accident, Janine cried. And she didn't stop. Her nose became plugged. Her eyes began to swell. Her dad unstrapped her from her chair, picked her up and carried her to her new bedroom. It was on the main floor where the computer room had been. He laid her on a brand-new bed.

Janine looked at her new room. A display case had been built into the wall. Her hockey trophies and medals gleamed as they caught the late-day rays of sunshine coming in through the window.

"Take the trophies away!" Janine continued to cry. "Dad, please, please, *please* empty that case!"

Mr. Burnett didn't reply. He left the room and didn't return. Janine cried herself to sleep.

PATIENT DIARY:

I never asked to be special. I just want my life back. I don't need people being nice to me.

And why do I have to make a statement to some court? Doesn't the wheelchair make enough of a statement?

I had to stop checking my Facebook page. You know how when someone dies, their Facebook page becomes like a memorial? People post old pictures and stuff. They write about what the person was like when they were alive.

Well my page is like that, lots of old photos and posts from people who feel sorry for me. But I'm not dead.

My Aunt Grace posted, "I will still love you." Like me being in a wheelchair might stop some people from caring about me? I mean, "I will still love you . . ." isn't that something you'd post if the person commits a crime or something?

I want them all to stop. But being at home for the first time since the accident makes me worry. I think it's gonna get worse before it gets better.

4 BACK TO THE BOOKS

Janine hated this . . . this *thing*.

It's not even a bus, she thought. *It's a van. A van with a big ramp that makes a big scene. Ugh.*

A boy with two canes across his lap was already in the van when it pulled up in front of her house.

Janine nodded and stared at her tablet. The boy said "hello," and that his name was Marlon.

She kept staring at the screen when he said, "I saw about you on TV. I'm really sorry."

She made a mental list of all the apps she needed to delete, when he said, "You know, we were in grade school at Westglen together."

Janine tried to stay focused on the screen. But she noticed that Marlon waved his hands when he was talking. And that he fixed his glasses a lot. What she really wanted was for Marlon to stop talking. Or for the van trip to end.

"I guess we'll be riding to school together," said Marlon. "Every day."

"Lucky us." Janine forced a smile.

"Ha, lucky us," Marlon snickered. "It's nice to have you to talk to. Once I get to class, everyone pretty well ignores me. I've had the canes for a long time."

"Yeah, I kind of remember that," said Janine. She thought that maybe Marlon might be happy and quiet down. She didn't get the result she wanted.

"Yeah, my spine is what the doctors call *misshapen*. Born that way. So, that's why I need . . ."

"Thanks for sharing," Janine said curtly.

"Okay, Janine," he said. "But if there's any time you ever want to talk . . . I mean, it would just be crazy, I mean crazy good, if you wanted to ask me anything. I'm happy to help you."

"Is there anyone else to pick up?" Janine called to the driver.

"No," the driver called back. "Just you two. Express service!"

"Is there anyone else who rides this van other days?"

"No," said the driver. "It's been just Marlon and me. But now it's the three of us."

"Okay, Marlon," Janine looked up from her tablet. "Some ground rules. In the morning, I like quiet time. You know? So, it's best if you give me my space, right?"

"For sure!" Marlon smiled. "Space. Got it. Can do."

The van pulled up to a driveway near the main door

of the school. Standing on the sidewalk, books cradled in her arms, was Rowena.

The driver pulled the van over, got out and slid open the side door. With the push of a button, a ramp unfolded and extended out of the van like a giant metal tongue.

First, the bus driver helped to wheel Janine down the ramp. Then Marlon ambled down, one arm through the loop in each cane. He leaned forward on the canes, picking them up one at a time to help him walk.

"Have a great day, Janine!" Marlon called out.

Janine's face turned a bright shade of red. "Space, Marlon. Remember? *Space.*"

Janine turned to Rowena. "What are you doing here?" she hissed.

"Um, maybe the accident robbed you of your memory. I go to school here," Rowena said.

"But did you have to wait for the special-needs van like some kind of welcoming service?" Janine moaned. "Why not hold up a sign with BURNETT on it like you're waiting for me at the airport?"

"I see that you're cheery this morning," Rowena shrugged. "Remember when we were like, eight, and we went on that camping trip with my parents? And we stayed up all night and made pinkie swears that we'd be friends for life?"

"Yes," Janine sighed.

"Pinkie swears trump everything. You know that. Friends for life."

Janine sighed and began to wheel her way to the door. "I feel like everyone in the school is looking at me."

"Newsflash," said Rowena. "They *are* all looking at you. And it'll be like this for a while. Then it'll all be same-old, same-old."

"It'll be same-old, same-old when I get out of this chair."

Janine pressed the silver Door Open button and one front door slowly opened. She rolled in to where Principal Chen was waiting for her.

"Welcome back, Janine." Principal Chen smiled. "If there's anything you need, come to the office and chat with me. I looked at your schedule. I see your first class is up on the second floor. The elevator should be easy for you to use."

"Thanks," Janine tried to force a smile.

"I'll go up with you," said Rowena.

Janine navigated the crowded hallways. When students heard the wheels squeaking, they moved closer to their lockers and gave her a path. The elevator was near the school's big side doors.

Janine pressed the Up button and the elevator doors slowly opened. A large pile of boxes took up almost half the space inside.

The school custodian ran up from behind.

"So sorry," he said. "Had a delivery of books today. I used this for quick storage. I'll move them later. There's still enough room for you, right?"

Janine nodded. She could roll herself in, but it was a tight squeeze. She had to reach behind a box to hit the 2 button.

"I guess I'll take the stairs," said Rowena. "I'll see you up there."

"I'll have that cleaned out later today!" the custodian called as the doors slowly began to close. "*So* sorry!"

5 BACK IN THE GAME?

PATIENT DIARY:

I have to ride in the stupid van. Just me and some other kid. He's really annoying. I can feel him staring at me to school and back home. I feel so big and bulky and stupid.

School is weird. When I come around, everyone stops talking. They nod, smile, ask how I'm doing. But they're all just waiting for me to go away. Everyone except for Rowena, who's taking the best-friend thing way too seriously. I mean, she's stalking me, making sure I'm okay. Oh, and I guess this Marlon guy, too. Maybe I can get Rowena to talk to Marlon. They can become friends. Then I can be left alone.

After a week at school, Janine was getting used to the elevator being half-filled with some shipment or the other. She was getting used to kids she didn't even know going out of their way to be polite to her. They held doors for her and they asked her if she needed help carrying her books.

On the van rides, she put on headphones. She tried to bury herself in a book and faked falling asleep to try to get Marlon to stop talking to her. None of it worked.

"I see you listening to your music again," Marlon said. "So, I made you a mix."

Janine turned up the volume. Maybe the music would drown out his voice.

"Check it out on your tablet. I'm Marlon123 on Spotify. I looked you up and made a friend request. I saw what kind of music you like."

Janine couldn't let it pass. She went to the Spotify app on her tablet. And there it was. A mix called *JANINE*. Fifteen songs. On the public sharing list! Anyone could see it!

"Marlon!" she barked.

"Your headphones are on too loud," he said. "You're yelling!"

"No, I'm yelling because I want you to delete this mix right now!" She ripped off the headphones.

"Look, I'm sorry," said Marlon. "It's just that you listen to your music so loud I can tell what kind of music you're into. I think anyone within, like, ten car lengths of this van can tell what music you're into. I just thought I could . . . well . . ."

Back in the Game?

"Okay, Marlon," Janine said icily. "Go on."

"It's normal to want to shut out everything and everybody. I get that."

"You don't know me, Marlon!" Janine hissed.

"Well, I kinda do. I mean, everyone in our school knows Janine Burnett."

"Yeah, the accident was in the news, all over the Internet."

"No, we all knew about the great Janine before that. Most popular member of the in-crowd. Hockey star. I remember that time you and your friend organized the drive for the food bank. Everyone lined up to help. It wasn't just because it was a good thing to do. It was what Janine wanted us to do. Popular kids aren't supposed to be nice. They're supposed to be jerks. But you were different. And now, you're mad. You have every right to be. So, you turn up the music and hope it all goes away. Look, I'm not as dumb as you think. You don't think I notice that when you look at me, you want me to disappear? I've been riding this van since kindergarten and there are still mornings I wake up mad. It's just the way it is."

"Marlon. Shut. Up."

Three and a half hours later, Janine finished her lunch. She wheeled herself out of the lunch room and down the hall toward the gym. It was as if the gym was calling to her.

Janine stopped just outside the gym doors. She heard

the slap of sticks and the squeak of running shoes on the polished floor. Before the accident, Janine and Rowena used to inhale their lunch. Then they would dash down to the open gym for pick-up floor hockey. Every day with their friends, girls and boys.

Now, it was lunch hour and Rowena was inside playing. The gym doors didn't have the big Open buttons, so Janine reached up and heaved on the handle as hard as she could.

Through the crack of the open door, she saw Rowena jumping off the bench and into the play. Rowena threw her shoulder into a guy who was six inches taller than she was. Rowena swiped at the ball with her stick, stopping a scoring chance for the other team.

Janine closed her eyes. She imagined she was banging her stick on the floor, screaming, "Pass it!"

She opened her eyes to watch Rowena spin away from a boy trying to reach the ball with his stick. Rowena laid a pass off for her teammate, who brought his stick through the ball, launching it several feet over the net.

The other team had the ball, and Rowena hunted for a bad pass attempt to pounce on. The ball went off a couple of sticks and rolled into the corner. Rowena chased after it, got it on the end of her stick, then fired the ball in front of the goal. It was deflected into the net by one of her teammates. Rowena raised her stick in the air.

Janine closed the door and wheeled away.

Back in the Game?

★ ★ ★

Janine waited on the school's front walk. Marlon sat on a nearby bench, his canes resting on his lap. The van was late.

"I saw you," Rowena said coming up the walkway.

"Saw what?" Janine said.

"Peeking through the door. Watching the game."

Janine shook her head.

"I saw you. You see, if you open the gym door even a crack, a wind comes in. We can all feel it."

"You still need to pick up your head when you play," Janine scolded. "Your head's down too much. One day you're gonna get creamed."

"Okay, Coach," Rowena rolled her eyes. "If you miss watching me play that much, you should come down Saturday for team practice."

"What?" said Janine. *Oh no, my team can't see me like this.* "I don't think it's a good idea."

"Why not?" Marlon looked up.

"Not like this, Marlon," Janine said, pointing down to her legs. "And who asked you?"

"Like what?" Marlon cried. "Are you ashamed or something? Trust me, you get over that. The worst part is when you realize that you've pushed all your friends away. I wish I would have had friends to push away, you know."

"No one asked you, Marlon!" Janine yelled. Her cheeks were getting red.

"Of course not, no one asks me anything," Marlon said. "I'm just the guy no one notices. Or the one people pretend not to notice. Then, one day, the coolest girl in the school ends up riding in my van."

"Wait," Janine hissed. "Are you saying you're *happy* that I'm stuck here with you?"

Marlon went silent. For a minute. Two minutes. He looked down at the ground. Then, he looked up and saw the headlights in the distance.

"I think the van is here."

6 AT THE RINK

Terwillegar Rec Centre was a complex in Edmonton's southern suburbs. It was like a small city. When it came to building mega-complexes, no other place in Canada came close to Edmonton. It had the biggest shopping mall in the country and a rec centre you needed a map to find your way around. A massive swimming pool with a water slide sat in the middle. Off that was a long hall lined with hockey rinks. Each rink had a wide glass wall, so people could watch the games. In the halls, screens like the ones that showed departures and arrivals in airports displayed which teams were playing in which rinks.

Janine wheeled through the doors that led directly to the hockey compound, her dad trailing her. There was no getting out of this. Coach S. had already talked to her dad. The Ice Devils wanted to see their team captain.

"I don't see why I have to do this," Janine said.

"It's getting close to playoff time," her dad said.

"We thought it might be a good idea for you to be around the team. You know, to inspire them."

"Well, let's make this quick," she said.

Her dad wheeled her to Pad 3. The Zamboni was just leaving the rink. The familiar smell of exhaust filled the air.

Janine saw Coach Sibierski in his black Ice Devils jacket skate onto the ice, a bucket of pucks in his hand. He dumped the pucks onto the ice and they made slapping noises as they scattered.

Then, one by one, her teammates came onto the ice. They were all wearing the god-awful pink practice jerseys that Janine had begged Coach S. to get rid of.

Janine's dad opened a door in the boards and wheeled Janine through the gap. Her teammates formed a semicircle around her, banging their sticks on the ice.

Coach S. skated forward. "Janine, good to see you."

Janine didn't know what to say, so she didn't say anything.

"Look, this season has been tough for all of us," said the coach. "But we're dedicating the rest of the season to you."

The girls smacked their sticks on the ice again.

Janine cleared her throat. "Well," she said. "If you're going to dedicate this playoff run to me, you'd better win, right? 'Cause it would suck if you lost."

Janine went back into the hallway to watch her

teammates practise, through the glass.

Rowena was still keeping her head down too long. Abby, the team's goalie, had to do better controlling her rebounds. Deborah still backed off too much when she defended.

"I'm not sure the team is where it needs to be, Dad," she said.

"Ever the critic," her dad said in her ear.

"Hey, you're the sports writer. You've been carving players for as long as I can remember."

"Yup," her dad said.

"You looking forward to getting back to work?" she asked.

"Sort of," her dad said. He watched Rowena's slap shot miss the net by five feet. "It'll be nice to be covering the team again. But the travel was tough before. It'll be even tougher now."

"We were used to it before," Janine said. "Mom and I will be fine."

Janine shivered. It wasn't because her dad was going back to work. It was because of how sloppy the Ice Devils looked on the ice. They missed passes. Their shots went wide. And when shots did find their way on target they went in, but only because the Ice Devils' goalies couldn't make saves.

"Honestly, Dad, they're terrible," said Janine. "This is nowhere near the team I played on."

"Well, you were their best player."

Were. Not 'is.' Or 'will be again.' Were.

Finally, Coach S. blew his whistle. The players came to a stop and then began collecting pucks and putting them in the buckets. Some of the players skated gentle laps around the ice to cool down.

Janine's dad wheeled her back through the doors and onto the ice.

"Say something encouraging," he whispered in her ear.

Coach S. skated over. He leaned over Janine's chair. In a hushed tone, he said, "Not so good, huh?"

"Everyone looked like it was their first time on the ice or something," said Janine.

The coach nodded.

One of the players quietly skated away to retrieve something from the bench. It was Janine's new number 94 sweater, the one she was supposed to wear this season. It was in a frame.

"Sorry there isn't more fanfare," said Coach S. "But we wanted to do something. Retiring your number seemed like a good idea."

Janine felt something. It wasn't joy or even sadness. Maybe it was anger. There it was again. Her number, retired. Janine's hockey career, officially over. Janine was once again being talked about in the past tense.

"Why can't we go home now?" Janine asked her dad. Practice was over. The Ice Devils were getting changed. The Zamboni slowly put a fresh gloss on the ice.

"Just wanted you to see one more thing," said her dad.

Rowena walked up and joined Janine where she sat with her dad and Coach S.

Janine looked back at the ice. What was that? Someone in a hockey jersey and helmet was sliding along the ice. But he was on a sled. Even through the glass, she could hear the long blades on the bottom of the sled shearing the ice. The player was strapped in, like a driver in a race car. In each hand was a mini hockey stick. One end of the stick had a small blade. What was that at the other end?

The player's movements answered Janine's question. He drove his right-hand stick into the ice, blade-side up. There was a chunking sound and then the sled whipped forward. Janine saw that there were picks on the other end of the stick. To move forward or backward, the rider used the picked ends to drive the stick into the ice. It was as if, in some bizarre way, he was steering a raft.

Then, more sleds appeared. The coaches strapped the players into them.

"Sledge hockey," said Coach S.

As more sleds started moving about on the ice, a woman skated out and dumped a bunch of pucks. Janine watched as the players used the bladed ends of the sticks to give and receive passes. Then they flipped over the sticks and drove the jagged, picked ends into the ice to pull themselves around. Sleds banged into each other with all the grace of a demolition derby.

"This is just the warm-up," said Coach S. "You should see what happens when the game starts."

"I think we should maybe watch a period, huh?" said Janine's dad.

Rowena and Coach S. nodded in agreement.

"Wait a second," Janine felt her anger rise up again. "This is hockey for crippled people!"

"No," said Coach S. "These teams allow able-bodied players, too. Sledge hockey is a game that happens to be accessible. Think of it that way."

"This was your plan all along!" Janine raged. "To show me this stupid sport!"

7 THE DEAL

Marlon had some home-baked cookies in his bag. The buttery aroma was almost too much to take. When he offered her one, she had to decide: accept a still-warm chocolate-chip-oatmeal cookie from Marlon and give him the satisfaction of doing something nice for her? Or ignore the gesture?

Janine knew she should have ignored Marlon. But she took the cookie. It was delicious. And when Marlon said, "you're welcome," she knew that she'd have to force herself to be nice to him for at least the rest of the day — and that included the ride home. *Ugh.*

Janine had been looking forward to this day all week. Her dad would be back in Edmonton after a long road trip with the pro team. She had hoped it would make that ride in the van with awful, awful Marlon at least bearable. It didn't.

Janine slipped her tablet into the case hooked to the side of her wheelchair. She wheeled herself into Mr. Massey's class and parked at her desk.

The other students were already at their desks. Mr. Massey was scribbling *ASSIGNMENT* on the whiteboard at the front of the class.

Janine thought he looked like every social studies teacher in Canada. Rumpled suit, jacket over a polo shirt. He wore a scarf with a red *CANADA* emblazoned on it. His beard was well trimmed. His glasses sat neatly on his face.

He turned to the class. "Ahem. I want each of you to think of career you'd like to know more about. And then we'll try to arrange for each of you to shadow people doing those jobs."

The class was silent.

Janine raised her hand.

"Yes, Janine?"

"Is it possible to not do this assignment?"

"Excuse me?" Mr. Massey offered the shocked, wide-eyed look that someone has when he or she has been punched.

"Yes," said Janine. "I mean, um, what job could I do?"

"How about sportswriter?" Mr. Massey's beard moved slightly as his chin moved upward and his lips squashed down. "Your dad is a mighty fine one. One of the best."

"Well, it's not a career that's gonna be around in twenty years, is it?" Janine replied. "Aren't sportswriters losing their jobs? Aren't newspapers closing down?"

The Deal

"Well, your dad has been going strong for as long as I can remember. I remember reading his columns when I was a kid."

Janine clenched her fist. *Why does Mr. Massey have to be like that?*

"Yeah, I guess," Janine said.

"Is there any chance you could shadow him? After all, you're such a hockey fan. I always just assumed the reason you wore hockey sweaters to school was because you were, well, Jack Burnett's daughter."

Janine gritted her teeth.

"Anyway, class," Mr. Massey said, surveying the room. "I'm sure that, if not your parents, then an uncle or an aunt or a friend's uncle or aunt does something you find interesting. I just want you all to report what it is like to spend a day on the job. And," Mr. Massey's gaze fell back on Janine. "Everyone has to do it. No exceptions. And Ms. Burnett needs to see me after class, please."

★ ★ ★

Janine's wheelchair was across the desk from Mr. Massey's beat-up brown chair. He didn't look up from the papers on his desk.

"So, Janine, do you think that was a good idea? You tried to wriggle out of an assignment, with the whole class watching."

Janine paused for a second. *Why does Mr. Massey have it in for me today?*

Mr. Massey shuffled his papers and looked up. "Judging by the fact that you haven't answered me, you don't have a good reason."

"No sir," Janine whispered.

"So, why is it that you don't want to job-shadow your father?"

"Look, sir, I don't want to shadow anyone. Why learn about careers?"

"To learn what it's like to have a job."

"But, I'll always need . . ."

"What?" Mr. Massey took his glasses off, wiped the lenses with a rag and put them back on. "You'll always need help? Well, I guess we all need help some of the time. That's life. But this isn't you trying to feel sorry for yourself, is it?"

"Is being realistic feeling sorry for myself?"

"Being realistic doesn't exclude you from doing this assignment, Janine. And it doesn't exclude you from having a job. Either ask your dad or find another job to shadow. What you choose is up to you. But, Janine, I expect your report on my desk when everyone else in the class submits theirs. Now, go."

★ ★ ★

The third stall in the girls' washroom on the main floor

was extra-wide for wheelchair access. In their first year of junior high, Rowena and Janine had dubbed it the Office. It was the place they went when they needed to have a quick talk.

Right after her second-period class, Janine's phone buzzed. It was a text message from Rowena.

Important. Office. Right after lunch bell.

After the bell went, Janine wheeled into the washroom. There were other girls there, but none went near the accessible stall. From a distance, Janine could see Rowena's blue and orange sneakers peeking out from under the door.

Janine tapped on the door. It opened. Janine's chair barely fit through the widened opening. Rowena shut the door behind Janine and closed the latch.

"So, what?" Janine whispered.

"Um, I heard about what you did in Mr. Massey's class," Rowena hissed. "I heard it from Treena Parker in second period. She said you said you didn't need to do your assignment, in front of the whole class."

"Yeah, okay, I did." Janine gestured at her wheelchair. "It's this stupid thing! This stupid accident! It used to be when I got angry, I'd save it for when I got on the ice! Now, it's all balled up inside."

Rowena leaned against the wall of the stall. "I'm guessing this would be the wrong time to ask you what you thought of the sledge hockey game we watched? To see if you'd give it a try? I'd go with you."

Janine shook her head. "Really? You're still on that? I watched their stupid game and it's done. Can't you all just leave me alone?"

"Well, you were the one saying you used to be able to take out all your anger on the ice. So maybe getting back on the ice might help calm you down. Save you from having more incidents like you had with Mr. Massey."

Rowena pulled her phone out of her pocket and began pounding on it with her thumbs. She turned the screen toward Janine.

Canada Beats Slovakia 3–2
Team Canada Celebrates Tournament Victory in Bratislava

Underneath was a picture of a player wearing Canadian national hockey team garb. The player was in a sled, with two sticks raised in the air.

"That's from this year's world championships," said Rowena. "It's a big deal. Hockey Canada sent a team and won gold."

Janine shook her head slowly. "Did you bookmark that and save it for when you needed to tell me to try out for the national team in a sport I've never played?"

"No," Rowena said. "I want you to be inspired. You've got to stop feeling sorry for yourself. You've got to get back on the ice. It's hockey. It's just played a different way. I looked it up. The Edmonton Athletics club welcomes new players of all skill levels. Disabled *and* able-bodied."

Janine's eyes narrowed. It looked like she was squinting. "You already called them, didn't you?"

"Maybe. To ask a few questions. Just, in general."

"You had no business doing that!"

"I do if I'm thinking of playing. Janine, we could go together. Play on the same line again. And you'd get to see me look like an idiot."

"However tempting that may be," said Janine. "No deal."

She turned, unlatched the door and rolled away.

PATIENT DIARY:

So, what is this, a conspiracy?

Rowena decides to bug me about sledge hockey. Again. When will she get the message I don't care about her idea?

I'm still getting sick to my stomach, literally. It's super frustrating. On the way back home in the van, I puked into a bag. Marlon told me not to worry about it. Barfing in front of Marlon — FAIL!

Stick Pick

I hate Marlon. He seems so happy that I'm right there with him in the van. When I do something embarrassing it makes him feel like I've been knocked right back to his level.

I HATE THIS!

8 GAME NIGHT

Janine could hear the roar of the crowd coming from underneath the press box. The noise wasn't all around her. It was somehow detached from where she sat. She was sitting next to her dad in the press box, which was located on the eighth floor, a level above the cheapest nosebleed seats in the arena. Two rows of seats and desks let journalists watch the game, with their laptops in front of them. The top row had booths for radio and TV announcers. Those in the press box had a bird's eye of the ice. Janine thought it was weird to look up and almost be able to touch the metal girders supporting the arena's roof.

A Los Angeles defenceman rocketed a shot on goal. It tipped off an Edmonton player in front of the net and went in over the goalie's shoulder.

Janine watched her father begin to type. He had happily agreed to let his daughter shadow him for a home game. His editor had arranged to get Janine a game pass to give her access to the press box and the teams' dressing rooms.

Stick Pick

Los Angeles won the face-off. They got the puck into the Edmonton zone and their players crashed the net. The goal light went on.

"Two to nothing already!" Janine blurted out. "They haven't even played a minute."

"Edmonton needs to win this game to stay close to L.A. in the standings," said her dad. "They can't afford to give up another goal . . ."

As if on cue, Los Angeles scored again, a two-on-one break that led to a puck going in the top corner. There was a *boo* from the crowd below and Edmonton's coach decided to change goalies.

Janine thought that Edmonton looked just like the Ice Devils: the missed passes, shots going off target, giving the puck away. But she didn't feel anything. She used to watch Edmonton games and agonize over every goal they surrendered, every penalty they took. She used to scour the Internet for stats.

But tonight, she thought to herself, *who cares?*

"Dad," she asked. "Do you ever wonder why people care so much if Edmonton wins or loses? Or why it matters who wins the Stanley Cup or a gold medal?"

Her dad looked up from his laptop. "That's a deep philosophical question, don't you think?"

"These fans don't know these players. They aren't cheering for their friends. Most of these players aren't even from Edmonton. Why do we care so much? Buying tickets and jerseys and cards and hoping to get an autograph? Getting sad when they lose and celebrating when they win?"

"Maybe it's because we all need to be part of something bigger than ourselves."

Janine shrugged as her dad resumed typing.

Is that why I didn't want to job-shadow my dad? Because I'm just not that excited to watch pro hockey anymore? But don't I love hockey more than anything?

The second period was slow. Edmonton got some long-range shots on goal. But they couldn't muster a goal. They unleashed shots from all angles at Mike Queen, Los Angeles' goaltender. Nothing got through.

Five minutes into the third period, the score hadn't changed. Janine's dad unplugged his laptop and put it into its case.

"We're going, now?" asked Janine.

"The media room is downstairs. We'll watch the rest of the game on the monitors in the media room, so we can zip to the dressing rooms right after."

They took the elevator down. Reporters were seated at tables, watching the game on monitors that lined the walls. Her father sat and opened his laptop.

"Wow, Jack, this one will be easy," said a reporter from across the room. Janine saw from his media pass that his name was Oscar. "What a gift. L.A. scores a bunch early and Edmonton can't do a thing."

Just as Oscar finished speaking, Janine heard the roar of the crowd through the walls. Then she watched the TV screen as an Edmonton player streaked down the ice and squeezed a shot through Queen's pads.

"The TV feed is a few seconds behind real time," explained her dad.

Then, another roar. Los Angeles had taken a penalty and Edmonton was on the power play. A few seconds later, after winning the face-off, the home team jammed home a second goal.

Oscar blurted out, "You have got to be kidding me!" just as a third roar rocked the media lounge.

Janine kept her eyes fixed on the TV screen. With the delay, she knew she was about to see the home team score again.

3–3!

The reporters in the room, including her dad, were typing frantically.

"It's exciting for fans. But comebacks like this are nightmares for us!" her dad panted. "We have to rewrite everything we've been working on all game long!"

And then came another roar, the loudest one yet.

Oscar pounded his fist on the table.

Confirmation came from the TV feed. With just ten seconds left, the home team had won it, after a wild scramble in front of the Los Angeles net.

Janine watched as her dad's fingers darted like lightning on the keyboard. At school, she'd get a week to write a 700-word assignment. Her dad was banging out a whole story in minutes.

Game Night

As soon as he hit send, he was up. "We have to get to the dressing room!"

Janine rolled her chair as fast as it would go. She was heading down a hallway, trying to keep up with her dad and a crowd of reporters and camera operators. He was moving at something between a brisk walk and a jog.

Oscar came running down the hall after them, wheezing. "Okay, Jack, same deal as usual?"

"Yup," her dad responded.

"The room is open!" cried a man in a suit at the end of the hall. The throng pressed forward. Oscar turned right and headed toward Los Angeles' dressing room. As Janine followed her dad into Edmonton's dressing room, the man who opened the room took a long look at her pass. "Yup, you're okay to go in," he said.

She went in, her phone in her hand. It was set to record so she could tape her interviews. She went looking for James McGee, the Edmonton player who had scored the overtime winner. He was standing in the middle of the dressing room. He wore a sweat-soaked blue T-shirt, shorts and flip-flops. Already, he was surrounded by reporters and cameras. As McGee spoke, her dad looked behind him and saw that Janine couldn't get inside the scrum. He grabbed her phone and held it toward McGee's lips, and returned the phone to Janine when the star player had stopped talking.

Next, reporters clamoured around Jussi Nieminen, who had scored two goals in the comeback. Janine tried to push through. But again, no luck. She felt like no one could see her.

Finally, the person who had let her in told her she could talk to Steven James, the team's goalie. "He's free right now," said the man, whose name tag showed he was the team's head of public relations. "You can do a one-on-one."

"Thanks," Janine said. She wheeled over to where James sat alone in the corner.

"Hi, you're new," the goalie said. He offered his sweaty hand for Janine to shake. His white pads were still on, making him look like a giant hunched in the dressing-room stall.

"So, um, tell me about the game tonight?" Janine started.

"Well, I got put in after we went down. I just tried to make sure their lead didn't get any bigger. It was a great comeback. Team effort."

Janine decided to ask about the thing that had been bothering her the whole game. "Do you ever wonder why so many people come to your games and cheer you on and buy your team's stuff?"

"Um, wow," the goalie put his hand to his chin. "Tough one. I mean, we love our fans, we play our hearts out for them . . . I mean, wow. That's a great question."

Game Night

★ ★ ★

Oscar burst into the media room, out of breath.

"I'll. Have. The. Quotes. In. A. Sec. Jack," he panted. "It was forever before their coach talked to us. And when he did, it was mostly swearing."

"I got the coach and a couple of players from the Edmonton room," Janine's dad said. "I'll e-mail you the best quotes as soon as I write them up."

"Dad," Janine said. "Let me know when we can go home."

"Soon," her dad said. "I have to get the stuff I got from the L.A. dressing room emailed to Oscar and then finish my write-up."

He sat down, put an earbud in his right ear and began typing up his interviews on his laptop.

9 HEART-TO-HEART

"So, you weren't excited or anything? You just wanted to go home?" Rowena stood in the corner of the Office. Janine's chair took up almost all the space in the stall. Rowena had to lean back against the bright orange wall.

"Really, it sucked," said Janine. "That press box is way up. I mean, give me an oxygen mask. We're looking way down to see the scoreboard that's hung over the ice. And everything is so, well, planned. Everyone splits up about who interviews who. They go in, talk to the players, and go out. I mean, it's all so, so, so . . . well, it feels kind of scripted."

Rowena sighed. "So, you're telling me you were frustrated? Bored?"

"I don't know. I think, deep down, despite everything, I still love hockey. But it felt weird. Like I was an outsider. Like I didn't belong."

"Maybe it's because you don't play anymore," said Rowena.

Janine shrugged. "You might be right. I'm never

going to play hockey again. That is, unless some miracle cure is found or something like that."

"But . . ."

Janine's nose crinkled up and she pursed her lips. She held her breath for a second before she spoke. "You are not going to go on about me playing sledge hockey, again."

"Yes, because you were the one who brought it up," Rowena smiled.

"No!" Janine said. "I am not going to play some game that is nothing but a pity party for cripples!"

"Wait a second," said Rowena. "Did I not offer to try the game out too? Do I look like I need a pity party? If it was such a pity game, why would we have provincial teams and a national team? I tell you, I watched videos of some of the games and the players didn't look like they were there just to feel good about themselves. There were collisions. Players got knocked around. When Canada scored, they celebrated like the whole world was watching."

"*Blah blah blah*," said Janine.

Rowena frowned. She slid along the wall of the stall. When she got to the door, she unlatched it and pushed it open. "Get out, Janine."

"What?"

"Get out of the Office. You say you don't want to play sledge hockey because it's a pity party. But, look at yourself. You tell me how hard it is to ride in the van with Marlon. Whine, whine, whine. How you don't want to do this and you don't want to do that. Whine, whine, whine. I try to be there for you and you go on like I'm the last person you want to see. So, really, haven't you been having your own pity party all along? Get out. I mean it. I'm tired of seeing you saying no to this and complain about that or try to get out of assignments. One day you'll figure out that it's just a chair. That you're still you."

"R-r-r-owena?" Janine's mouth hung wide open. *What is this? What's come over her?*

"Look, I'm not saying you have to try sledge hockey. I'm not saying you have to like everything you used to like. But stop with the excuses, already. Get out, Janine."

"You have no idea what it's like to be me!" Janine cried. "That I can't do the one thing I loved more than anything!"

"Then find something else to love! Don't just mope about what you've lost. Maybe it's sledge hockey. Maybe it's writing stories like your dad. I don't know. But doing nothing, that's always going to suck. I mean it, Janine, get out!" She held the door open.

Janine slowly backed her wheelchair through the doorway. Rowena slammed it shut behind her. Janine wheeled across the bathroom tile, past the sinks and toward the exit. As she got to the door, she stopped. She spun and turned back toward the Office.

"So, you think I'm a big pity party all to myself,

huh?" she screamed at the closed bathroom stall. "You don't know what it's like to go to bed mad and wake up mad! You want me to come out and try this stupid sledge hockey? Fine! But I am so going to cream you! I am going to remember what you said. And I am going to hurt you on the ice. I swear, I will!"

The door opened slowly. Rowena pulled her tablet out of her bag and began typing and swiping. "Okay, then, the website says there is a skate on Saturday. Beginners welcome. So, we're going then. Right?"

"Whatever. Sure. Yes." Janine exhaled deeply.

"All right, then!" Rowena's frown transformed into a smile. "Looking forward to it!"

★ ★ ★

"So, you're the one who called about a tryout?" The woman was wearing a blue EDMONTON ATHLETICS jacket. She had matted black hair and deep wrinkles around her jet-black eyes.

"No, my friend did," said Janine. She wheeled closer to the opening in the boards. A couple of hockey sleds sat on the ice, their metal frames reflecting the blue-tinted lights of the Leduc Arena. Rowena stood behind Janine.

"Always happy to give a player, or a couple of players, the chance to try out the sport," said the woman.

"You're Coach Laboucaine? The one I talked to on the phone?" asked Rowena.

"Yup, but just call me Abby. In fact, the players call me Dear Abby because of my gentle disposition. Ha!"

Rowena gave a weak smile. Janine could tell that the coach was anything but sweet.

"So, there are the sleds out there," the coach continued. "I tried to set the length based on the heights you gave me over the phone. I might have to adjust the bars. I set the blades as far apart as I could. You won't go as fast, but it'll be easier to keep your balance."

"But I know how to skate," said Janine.

"You mean, you *knew* how to skate, on your feet," snorted Dear Abby. "But this is skating with your butt in a plastic bucket mounted on a sled. Totally different. Kid, you're gonna fall and make a darned fool of yourself. But we've got some other players coming out who will help you.

"And you." The coach turned to Rowena. "You're going to really struggle out there, Princess."

"What?" said Rowena.

"Well, look at how you and your friend are dressed. You're wearing those big, bulky shoulder pads. Didn't you get the memo? You're going to be moving these sleds with your arm power. Okay, show me how ready you are. Lower yourselves into your sleds and strap in."

Janine sighed. This was going to be a long day.

10 ON THE ICE

Coach Laboucaine turned and yelled "*Ryan!*" as loudly as she could. The syllables *Ry* and *an* echoed through the arena, over and over.

A boy about the same age as Janine and Rowena walked onto the ice. He was wearing a bright blue hockey jersey and the shortest hockey gloves Janine had ever seen.

"Ryan," Coach Laboucaine said, "can you show these two how to get set up in a sledge?"

"Okay," Ryan nodded. He looked at the girls. "My sled is right there next to yours. I'll show you."

"So, who are you escorting?" Janine asked.

"Escorting?" Ryan shrugged. "Oh, I get what you mean. I'm not escorting anyone. I'm on the team. I've found this is a great way to build upper body strength. Really helps me when I play hockey with my junior team."

"So, you play sledge hockey *and* regular hockey?"

Ryan laughed. "Well, if you want to call it *regular*

hockey, you can. I guess I used to think that way, too. But, after playing both, I'll tell you that they are both just *hockey*, but played different ways. My old triple-A coach suggested I try out sledge hockey to build my upper body strength. Boy, was he right! And now, I just like to play."

Ryan eased himself into his sled. He had to squeeze into the bucket. His feet pointed out, with his toes almost touching the metal nose of the sled. "Okay, you two," he said. "You're going to want to be in your bucket, strapped in as tight as you can."

Rowena sat in the bucket and did up the straps around her chest. With the coach's help, Janine lowered herself from her chair into the bucket. The coach did up her straps.

"Hey!" Janine said. "That's too tight. I can't breathe!"

"You know what?" the coach said. "That's as tight as it can go and it's still not snug enough. Your butt is going to slide around in that bucket. Did you bring extra cushions like I wrote in the email?"

Janine had a cushion she sat on in the wheelchair and an extra one tucked into the shelf below. Coach Laboucaine grabbed the bigger, fluffier pillow.

"This pillow's got bunny rabbits on it. How cute," she chuckled. She undid the strap on Janine's sled and ordered Janine to pick herself out of her bucket, just a little. Janine pushed on her hands to raise herself out of the seat. The coach shoved the cushion underneath Janine and ordered her to lower herself again.

Even with no feeling in her legs, Janine could tell how tightly she was packed inside the bucket once the strap was done up again. Her legs came forward and rested on the nose of the sled.

"You," the coach said to Rowena. "Tighten your strap. I can see you bobbing in that bucket."

"I think I'm good," Rowena said. Her voice wasn't much louder than a whisper.

"Good?" the coach crouched down and shook Rowena's sled. Janine could see Rowena slide back and forth in the seat. "We'll see how good you are when you try to make your first turn and the sled goes over sideways. Or the first time you crash into another sled. You think you're good? Your funeral, sweetheart."

"I remember the first time I played," Ryan said. "I was just like you. I thought I should be loosey-goosey in the bucket. Even when I wear skates, I tie them up as tight as they can go. Same idea, really. The tighter it is, the better your balance. But, no, I wanted to be comfortable in that bucket. I tipped over so many times, it was embarrassing."

Other players were getting into their sleds and moving around the ice. They propelled themselves using the spiked ends of the sticks. Even with their hockey jerseys on, Janine could see how huge their arms were.

"Okay, over here," the coach snapped her fingers.

"We're not done yet. Next thing you need to do is pick a stick. Long or short blade?"

"Long," Janine and Rowena said in unison.

"You'll be changing your mind about that soon enough," the coach sighed. She walked toward the bench and grabbed a bundle of sticks. She handed a pair to each player.

Ryan slid over so his sled was next to the two girls. "Let's see how you get around on the ice," he said. "Use the picked end of the stick to push the sled forward. Brace on one stick to turn. Watch me."

Ryan pushed both sticks down and pushed off. Then again. And again. It was like a drummer keeping the beat. He sped away. Then he pushed his right stick over and over into the ice to slowly make a sharp left turn toward the boards.

"Push on one side, and you'll turn the other way!" he yelled. "But to start, just try to get moving!"

Janine and Rowena started at centre ice. They drove their sticks — picked ends down — into the ice. Rowena drifted a bit to the left.

"You!" Ryan called out. "You must be right-handed!"

"Yes, why?" Rowena called back.

"I've seen it before. A right-handed person drives the right stick in just a little harder than the left. So, the sled drifts a bit left!"

Rowena and Janine moved toward the blue line. A sled came from the other end of the rink. It blew past them and got to the line well before they did.

"This . . . isn't . . . easy . . ." Rowena puffed as they got to their goal. "My arms, this is all on my arms."

Janine felt the burn in her arms. But she knew it wasn't as bad as the pain Rowena was feeling.

"I've been moving around in my chair for a few months," she said. "I've been building up my arm strength. But, yeah, this isn't easy."

Another quick-moving sled came close. It made contact with Rowena's sled as it went by. It was only a slight touch, but it was enough to shift Rowena in her seat.

And then her sled fell on its side.

"Help!" Rowena cried.

The coach slowly made her way over. She crouched down and looked Rowena in the eye. "Maybe you want to listen to me about strapping yourself in as tight as you can?"

"Yes, ma'am," Rowena said, hanging sideways out of the up-ended sled.

★ ★ ★

Janine got to the point where she could push off and turn in the sled. There were pucks all over the ice. She got to one that sat near a goal crease.

Rowena struggled to keep up. She'd fallen over a couple more times. Each time, the coach strapped her in a bit tighter.

Stick Pick

Ryan was practising his shooting. He stretched out his right arm and whipped his blade through the puck. It went into the top corner of the net. And then he did it again. And again.

Janine flipped over the stick so that the blade side was on the ice. The puck nestled against the long blade. She flicked her wrist, trying to send the puck on net. It moved about six inches. Sideways.

"Ha!" the coach cried. "I saw that! It's hard to control the puck with a long blade. Try the shorter blade. You'll find you can control and pass and shoot. And those hockey gloves you're wearing. Too bulky! You need lighter gloves, without the big cuffs."

The coach handed Janine two sticks with shorter blades. Janine took them and gave her the long-bladed sticks back.

Ryan passed a puck toward Janine. This time she was able to handle it. She could feel the puck on the end of the stick. She saw that Rowena was close by, so she slid a pass toward her friend's sled.

Rowena reached down to take the pass. The puck hit the long blade of her stick and bounced away. Rowena's sled rocked, but at least she didn't fall over.

The coach blew her whistle. "Okay, you two. Believe it or not, for the first time, you weren't terrible. Don't get me wrong, you're both bad. But, if you want to try this again, you're welcome to come out."

11 STAIRCASES AND STOREROOMS

Attention: Crown Prosecutor L.H. Beleski

Edmonton Law Courts, Churchill Square

VICTIM IMPACT STATEMENT: Janine Anna Burnett, Edmonton, Alberta, Canada

What has my life been like since the accident?

Well, I don't remember much about the actual accident. I sort of recall that we were on the highway talking about the tournament my team had just won. Then there were dreams and shapes and shadows. And then I woke up on a bed with a bunch of tubes stuck in me.

(For the record, needles suck.)

Since then, what has life been like? Everywhere I go, everyone gets this look on their faces. It's like, "I feel so sorry for you." They don't actually talk to me or anything. And if I look up at them I can see how quickly they look away.

Stick Pick

I get to ride in the special-needs van every morning and afternoon. Fun!

But it's not about me. Before, I was afraid to write about this, but to heck with it. My mom has changed. She'll always have to walk with a cane. But that's not all. She's obsessed with the court case. She never smiles. It's always "justice this" and "justice that."

I used to play hockey, and I loved it. My friend convinced me to try sledge hockey, and it's different. Everything in my life has changed.

Sometimes, I lie awake at night and wonder if it would be easier if we'd all been killed in the crash. Does that make me a victim?

I know the person who caused the accident might have to spend some time in jail. But I get to be in this chair for the rest of my life. No matter what happens, I am the one with the life sentence.

Mauro's was in a strip mall in Crestwood. Janine's parents couldn't possibly hope to afford a home in the tree-lined Edmonton neighbourhood filled with large homes. Her dad pulled the minivan into the parking lot. All three spots marked with blue disabled parking signs were taken. A large pick-up truck in one of the spots was running. A blue-grey plume of smoke hovered near its exhaust pipe. A man sat in the cab. The music he was listening to was so loud the bass shook the Burnetts' car, even through the truck's closed windows.

"He doesn't have a sign in his window that I can see. I don't think he can park there," said Janine's dad. He pulled up behind the truck and honked the horn.

Nothing.

Janine's dad pressed down on the horn again. And again.

Finally, the truck's window rolled down and the driver's head popped out. Janine's dad rolled down his window, letting in the bitter cold.

"Yeah, what?" the driver said.

"Can you please move your truck?" asked Janine's dad.

"Why?"

"Because we have a disabled parking permit. We'd like to use that spot."

"Sorry," the driver raised his bushy eyebrow. "But can you wait a sec? My wife is in the store right there and she'll be back in two shakes. We'll clear out of your way in a minute."

"Excuse me!" Janine's dad raised his voice. "You'll move it, now!"

But the driver of the truck had already rolled up his window.

So, Janine and her family waited. And waited. Finally, after fifteen minutes, a woman ran out of the store that was next to Mauro's. She had two well-filled shopping bags in her hands.

Finally, the truck backed out. The driver even gave Janine's dad a wave as he drove off.

"It's okay, dad," Janine said. "We're finally here. Time to get some spaghetti Bolognese. Time for our first family dinner out since . . . well, I can't remember when!"

The spaghetti Bolognese from Mauro's was Janine's favourite dish. She loved it with lots of garlic toast.

Janine slid into her wheelchair and then rolled down the ramp to the snowy parking lot. Her mom was waiting on the sidewalk. There were two small steps leading up to the door of Mauro's, both covered in ice. But there was a wheelchair lift right next to them.

On it was a sign: Out of Order.

"Oh, that's not right," Janine's dad said. "I'll go in and get them to help you up the stairs."

Her father disappeared into the restaurant. He came out two minutes later. His face was red. "I can't believe it!" he growled.

"What is it?" asked Janine's mom.

"They say they can't carry her up the stairs. If someone slips, they could get sued. They don't want to take that chance. They said the lift has been out of order for weeks! Weeks!"

"Jack, you and I could lift her up," said Janine's mom.

"I told them we could do that, and they said no way. They don't want us slipping and falling on their icy steps and then suing them! Basically, their attitude is that it's better luck next time."

★ ★ ★

Janine dug into her second-favourite dish, lemon chicken, at the Chinese restaurant on 97th Street. The sticky glaze was sweet and salty at the same time. Having it alongside the *special* rice, with peas and baby corn and chunks of ham, was pretty good, even if it wasn't spaghetti Bolognese.

Because it was a special day, her parents had allowed her a cola. And when she was finished one glass, the server would take it and return with another filled to the brim.

As she ate the last morsels of the lemon chicken, Janine realized she had to use the bathroom. The restaurant had washrooms downstairs. But it also had a family/accessible washroom clearly marked on the main floor, by the kitchen.

Janine excused herself and wheeled down a hall toward the accessible washroom. She opened the door. The automatic lights came to life.

There was a toilet and a sink at the other end of the large room. But to get there, Janine had to navigate through a maze of boxes. Some were marked Cleaning Supplies. Some were marked Plastic Cutlery. Others were marked Gloves. Chairs were stacked and leaning against another wall.

Stick Pick

To make room to get through, Janine had to nudge some of the boxes out of the way with her chair. A box that had been perched on top of two others came tumbling down. It broke open and bottles of bright pink cleaning fluid rolled across the floor. The bottles went here, there and everywhere. They cut off Janine's route back to the door.

Janine did the only thing she could do. She cried for help at the top of her lungs.

★ ★ ★

Janine sat in the back of the van, her head buried in her hands.

"Maybe we shouldn't go out ever again," she said. "No more celebrations."

"Bright side," said her dad. "When the manager finally got the door open, he was so embarrassed, we didn't have to pay for dinner. We might never have to pay for dinner at that restaurant again."

"He said no one ever uses that bathroom," snapped Janine's mom. "So, everyone thought it was all right to use it as a storeroom. We should sue. We deserve more than free meals."

"Oh, Mom, they felt bad enough," Janine said. "Does everything have to involve us going to court?"

"You're the one who wrote that she wondered if it was better if we'd all died," her mom said quietly.

She looked straight out the window. "The prosecutor forwarded what you wrote in the victim impact statement to me."

"Can we stop this?" her dad growled. "We were supposed to be celebrating tonight!"

"Whoopee," Janine said.

12 THE REPORT

As the bell rang, Mr. Massey asked, "Janine, can you stay behind for a couple of minutes?"

"Sure," Janine nodded. "I don't have class in the next period."

Her classmates filed out, leaving her alone in class with the teacher. She wheeled up to his desk.

He reached into his old tan leather satchel and pulled out her report.

"Interesting," he said. "I thought you were going to write a report like the ones your dad writes for the paper. After all, that was the whole point of shadowing, right?"

"Um, no," she said. "Sorry, what I mean is that I was *planning* to write a game report like my dad would write. But as the night went on, I thought there was something more important to write about, at least for me."

She looked down at the title page of her paper sitting on Mr. Massey's desk. The title, "Access for All?" was circled in red. Her teacher picked it up again.

"I'd like to ask you about this first page," he said. "This is what you wrote . . ."

JOB-SHADOW REPORT

SUBMITTED TO: MR. MASSEY, GRADE 8 SOCIAL STUDIES

BY: JANINE BURNETT

The disabled are told over and over that we will be afforded the same chances as everyone else. But this simply isn't true. I learned this as I covered my very first pro hockey game. Despite the best efforts of those who built the arena and the staff, the system doesn't really allow someone like myself to have equal opportunity.

You get a window of maybe a couple of minutes to get your interviews. Just getting from the media room and down a long hallway that goes underneath the stands takes time. In the dressing room, the players talk to all the reporters in large media "scrums." I couldn't get close to most players, I was squeezed out.

"Um, and?" Janine asked.

"You didn't write a game report. You wrote a report about what it was like to cover the game. Okay, fine. But I found that you didn't go deep enough. You write about how hard it was to get around. But you don't go into detail about what you'd change. You need to explore that in your piece. Don't dance around it."

"Sorry," said Janine. "I just thought I might get my dad in trouble."

"Why don't you talk to him about it and let him decide," said Mr. Massey.

★ ★ ★

That evening, over dinner, Janine told her dad what Mr. Massey had said.

"He wants me to write another draft," she said. "He told me he thought the paper could be great, that I just needed to be honest. But I was worried that if it got out, you could get into trouble."

Janine's dad laughed. "Janine, maybe your teacher is right. A good journalist always gives as many facts as possible to the reader. Do you know how many times I've ticked off the hockey team's front office? How many times a general manager or coach has growled to me about my work? I'm always in the crosshairs."

The Report

"Oh," Janine said. "I just thought it was nice of the team to give me a media pass and . . ."

"That's not how journalists look at it. Our job is to serve our readers. That's it. The team understands that we write about the good and the bad. It's just the job we have to do."

Janine's mom cut in. "Okay, enough about that. Janine, the Crown Prosecutor called today. She said she wants more about how the injuries will affect you long-term. Basically, your impact statement isn't long enough either."

Janine sighed. "What, everyone needs more sentences on why my life generally sucks now? Is there anything else?"

"Janine," her mother's eyes narrowed. "I will never walk properly again. You, well . . . anyway."

"Say it mom. 'Paralyzed from the waist down.' Not so hard."

"Well, okay. I mean, our lives have changed. The driver, this James Colangelo guy, he's going to plead guilty. That's what the Crown says. She says we'll need to have the statements for the judge, for sentencing."

"So? What do you want from me?"

"To write it again. Tell everyone about what you have to go through every day since the accident."

JOB-SHADOW REPORT (REWRITE)

SUBMITTED TO: MR. MASSEY, GRADE 8 SOCIAL STUDIES

BY: JANINE BURNETT

I wheeled into the dressing room, expecting to get the same access everyone else had. After all, it was a big, open room. No stairs. The players were all there, willing to be interviewed. But the rest of the reporters scrummed around all the stars of the game, and wouldn't let me in. They didn't care if I said "excuse me." If I tried to push my way in, they pushed me out.

I have found that making something accessible is one thing in theory, but it's totally another thing in practice. You can take away stairs and replace them with ramps. You can make rooms wide. But you can't change the way people think and act. And that's the problem. What good is an accessible doorway if someone blocks it off with boxes? What good is an accessible ramp if a bunch of people stand on it and block the way?

We parked downtown, a couple of blocks from the arena. It had snowed earlier, so it was hard for me to wheel down the sidewalk. The snow had been removed, but the path wasn't wide enough for my chair. And when I had to cross the street, there were large snowbanks on the curbs. My dad had to push me as hard as he could to get me through. What if I'd been on my own?

Once again, Mr. Massey asked Janine to stay after class. But this time there were no red circles on the first page.

"I think your new version is very powerful," he started.

"Thank you," said Janine.

"I think it deserves to be read by more than just your junior-high social studies teacher."

"Well, I don't know . . ."

Mr. Massey cleared his throat. "Janine, can I be completely honest with you?"

"Yes."

"Before your accident, you were the most confident girl in this whole school. If you didn't like something, you spoke your mind. Don't lose that."

"Mr. Massey, it's hard to try to stand out when you always feel like you need to apologize for yourself. Respectfully, try sitting in a chair like this, even for an hour. See how the whole world changes for you."

13 CONFRONTATION

Janine had the puck on her stick. Rowena was grunting from the strain of trying to keep up. Janine dug the picked end of her stick into the ice so she could turn to see just how far Rowena was behind her.

And then Janine was rocked. Her sled shook. She felt her chest strain against the straps as she heaved forward.

"Enough baby-feeding you," said the player whose sled had just crashed into Janine's.

As the player pushed her sled away, the picked end of one of her sticks raked across Janine's arm. Janine saw specks of blood on the sleeve of her white hockey jersey before she could register the pain.

"You have to watch yourself out there!" sneered the girl. "You and your friend are clogging up the ice. From now on, if you get in the way, you get hit."

Oh why, oh why did I agree to come back? Janine thought. *I thought for sure after the first practice Rowena wouldn't want to play anymore. What is wrong with us?*

Confrontation

Janine looked back to see if Coach Laboucaine had seen her getting spiked. The coach looked straight at Janine — and smiled.

"Get moving, Burnett!" she cried. "Is one hit gonna stop you? Are you gonna go home and cry to your mommy and daddy?"

Janine moved her sled away from centre ice. Out of the corner of her eye she saw Rowena's sled sliding backward from the force of a collision. The player had struck again.

Janine felt her blood boil. She barrelled toward the player. She pushed off so hard that the sled tilted a bit and, for a second, Janine thought she might fall over. But the sled righted itself and Janine was off in pursuit. Her arms burned from the effort.

Janine was going as hard as she could. But there was no way she could catch her quarry. The girl was too fast. Suddenly, she turned around and came bearing down on Janine's sled.

Crash. Harder than the first time.

"I guess you want some more, huh, hockey star?" said the other girl.

"Hockey star!" cried Janine. "What the heck does that mean?"

"Come on," said the other girl. "You don't think we don't recognize your face from the news? The little hockey expert who was in the accident. She feels so sorry for herself. Daddy and Mommy are going to court. They're gonna get a big settlement and everyone's gonna live happily ever after. Now you show up here and slide around and act like you can just hold everyone else up."

Janine was so angry, she took her stick and chopped the other girl on the arm. The other girl cried out. Coach Laboucaine blew her whistle.

"Okay, you two. Cool off. Both of you, take your sleds over to the boards and take a break."

Janine could barely restrain herself from giving the other girl another chop as she followed her to the boards.

"What was that about?" Janine hissed, as they parked their sleds.

"Oh, Janine Burnett is all angry," said the girl. "You *do* have emotions other than self-pity. What, you going to try and chop me again? I let you get away with that one. Do it again and I'll rake you with the picks so bad that they'll think you've been in a fight with a mountain lion."

"You think you know me?"

"I know your type. You come in and because you're new, you think it makes you better than the rest of us."

Ryan's sled screeched to a halt in front of Janine and her rival. A fine spray of snow flew from the blades of his sled as it came to a standstill.

"Sandy, what's with you?" he said. "Janine is just learning the game. You didn't have to target her like that."

Confrontation

He turned his head toward Janine. "This is Sandy. She's a good player. But she's always got to show the newbies that she's *sooooo* tough. She's all right once you get to know her. Now, Sandy, take off your glove, pull right up to the side of Janine's sled and shake hands."

"Beat it, Ryan," Sandy growled.

Ryan's eyes narrowed. "Janine, did you know that I've caught Sandy looking at videos of cute kittens on her tablet?"

Sandy drove one of her sticks into the ice. "Ryan! Stop that!"

"I will tell Janine a lot more about how sweet you really are if you don't shake hands."

Sandy grunted. She took the glove off her right hand and held it out for Janine to shake. "My name is Sandy. Sandy Tranh. I've been playing for six years, now. I see you're still wearing the big, bulky gloves. That's stupid."

Janine swallowed hard and didn't say a word.

Sandy laughed. "Talk much? You needed to be knocked down a peg. All the rookies do. Okay, that chop of yours is going to leave a mark. You got your shot in. Trust me, you do it again, I'll mess you up bad. And, if you want to start playing for real in summer league, you can go up against a junior on the Sherwood Park squad we call The Chopper. I don't know her real name. She's vicious. And the way she drives her sled, it's like a non-stop crash-a-thon. That's when you'll know what it's really like to get hit. What I am trying to say is, don't think this is where a bunch of us get together and feel sorry for ourselves and everyone goes home happy when the game ends in a tie. You come onto the ice, you get ready to play."

Coach Laboucaine blew her whistle. Through Rowena's helmet, Janine could see the greenish colour of her face. Janine had never seen her friend look that way. Rowena gasped for breath as she slid by. She tried to use her arms to lift herself out of the sled, but couldn't.

"So tired. My arms hurt. Bad. So. Bad." Rowena struggled to speak.

Janine watched as Sandy, using only her arms for leverage, lifted herself a foot and a half out of the bucket and into her wheelchair.

"I can't do that," Janine said.

"Play this game long enough and you'll get the strength to do it," said Sandy. "Does your friend need CPR or something?"

14 THE PRESENTATION

Mr. Massey stood in front of the social studies class.

"It's Janine's turn to present her paper. I'm asking you to be respectful and attentive. Janine, the floor is yours."

As Janine rolled to the front of the class, Mr. Massey took a seat behind his desk.

Janine spun to face the class.

"Um, hi, everyone," she said. She felt the blood rush to her face. "My job-shadow, well, it was my dad. Some of you might know he's a sportswriter. He travels across the continent writing about hockey. I think it's because of him that I fell in love with hockey when I was just a little kid."

She cleared her throat and looked back at Mr. Massey. He nodded.

"I expected to go to a game with my dad. I expected to see how cool it was to report on a game. Instead, it was all about being in a hurry, rushing here and rushing there. And, for me . . . you may have noticed I've been in accident."

87

There were some chuckles in the class. Others tried to stifle their laughter, not sure if it was okay to react to the joke.

Janine continued. "The pro hockey arena is built to be accessible. But I found that access has more to do with the people around you. So, people are bunched up around the hockey players. And you have to sprint to the dressing room to get quotes after the game. And there isn't time to get to both teams. All that makes the job hard enough for a person who can run. It's almost impossible for someone who is in a wheelchair. For example, the hallway leading into the media area isn't very wide. It's just wide enough for two thin people to walk by each other. My chair is wide and bulky — I took up the whole space.

"I do think the designers tried to make the place as accessible as possible. But they didn't realize that someone in a wheelchair might actually be working there. That they might need to speed from one spot in the arena to the other and get to a dressing room within minutes of a game ending. You can't make other people around you make way for you. At the mall, there's one elevator in the whole place, and there's a sign on it that says *For families with strollers and disabled patrons*. But the elevator is filled with people who could have used the stairs or the escalator. I had to wait, like, for three or four rides before I can get on.

The Presentation

"And on the bus, there's disabled seating in the front. But no one wants to get up from those seats when someone who is disabled gets on the bus. They give you dirty looks like you're doing it on purpose to make things harder for them.

"It all got me thinking. There are a lot of places where people think things are accessible for someone in a wheelchair, but they're not. I went to a restaurant and the accessible bathroom was filled with boxes. When I go out in the snow, people are good about cleaning their sidewalks, but they leave giant snowbanks that I can't get through. There are snow piles in the middle of the street that I can't hop over.

"I'll show you an example." Janine turned to the teacher behind her. "Mr. Massey, is it okay if everyone follows me out into the hall?"

He shrugged. "I want to see where you're going with this, Janine. The class is yours. Please, everyone form a line and follow Janine."

Janine opened the door slowly and rolled into the hall. Her classmates followed her out, with Mr. Massey at the end. Her wheels squeaked as they rolled on the freshly waxed floor. She came to a set of doors that led outside.

"Okay, everyone. These doors are automatic, right?" she said. "The round, silver button with the wheelchair logo is there on the side to activate the door."

Janine saw some of her classmates nod.

She manoeuvred her chair to the side of the doorway. She reached out. "But they put the button at a height for a person to reach if she was standing, not sitting. I've got to get someone to help me get to the button. Or I have to stretch my arm till it feels like my rotator cuff is gonna pop."

Her classmates were quiet.

"Follow me." She wheeled off to her left and down another hallway. The class followed her. She finished her journey at the doors to the elevator.

"So, any of you take the elevator?" she asked. No one said anything.

"I didn't think so. The elevator is kinda out of the way. And it's so slow that it's quicker to take the stairs. But I have something to show you."

She hit the Up button. The elevator doors opened. Inside the car were piles of boxes.

"It never fails. Deliveries get left in here. Someone sticks boxes of whatever in here to get them out of the way, thinking no one actually uses this elevator. I can barely squeeze in. It's like this all the time."

Janine wheeled away from the elevator and everyone followed.

Back in the classroom. Janine returned to the spot at the front of the class.

"There's one last thing I want to say. The reason a lot of people use accessible bathrooms as storerooms is because, well, they don't really *see* us. Most of you look at me, and if I look back you turn your head away. Don't think I don't notice. Or some people are way too polite now, like they're afraid to tell me a joke or talk to me like a real person. I'm still me. I just can't walk anymore. Don't be afraid to treat me like you used to. But, understand that I am here and sometimes I need you to make room. That's all."

Janine wheeled back to her desk. But, what was that sound? It was one of her classmates, standing up behind his desk and clapping. And then another. And then all of them stood up.

15 PLAYOFFS

Janine had the puck on her stick. She knew the hit was coming. Sandy was bearing down on her, fast. Janine passed the puck to a teammate before Sandy's sled crunched into hers.

"Okay, John!" Janine yelled, "get to the net!"

As Sandy and Janine separated, Sandy gave a small tap of the stick on Janine's sled. There was a slight ting.

"Good thing you got that pass off, Rookie," Sandy called out.

Rowena was in the corner, slowly getting back into the play after colliding with another player.

"You've got to get on your horse, Rowena!" called out Coach Laboucaine. "I'm trying to get you ready for the summer hockey season. You're gonna get eaten alive out there if you're sitting still!"

Rowena dug her picks into the ice and moved forward. The puck rolled into her area. She was able to reach down, corral it and launch a shot toward the goal. It hit a sled in front, bobbled around and then was cleared away by a defender.

Ryan slid by Rowena. "It's okay, I remember when I first started. I thought my arms were gonna fall off, they burned so much."

The puck rolled out to the blue line, close to Janine. She pushed forward, trying to turn left with one stick and corral the puck with the other. The puck nuzzled against the tape of her stick blade. She pushed down on the blade, forcing the puck to flatten to the ice. Janine took a swing and sent the puck back toward the crowd of players in front of the net. She heard the ring as it hit sled tubes. And then came a smacking sound as her stick blade hit the puck. She never saw how the puck went into the net, but her teammates raised their sticks in the air.

"Not bad, Janine!" Coach Laboucaine called out and then blew on her whistle. "Not bad at all. Get the puck to the traffic in front of the net and see what happens."

I better not tell her I'm not sure I meant to do that, thought Janine.

On cue, Sandy stopped in front of Janine. "You're not fooling me. You don't really know what you're doing out there. You got lucky."

"Okay, everyone, scrimmage over," the coach called out. "For those of you on the first team, be here early Saturday. This decides our season. It's either Sherwood Park or us. As for the rest of you, including our two latest recruits, well, I did see some progress. You still look scared out there, though."

★ ★ ★

Rowena and Janine sat next to each other in the lobby of the Leduc Arena. Their teammates were with them.

"Coming to watch our big game against Sherwood Park, Rookie?" Sandy asked.

Wait, she's talking to me? What do I do? Janine thought. "Well, um, you see . . ."

"Spit it out, Rookie."

"I'd like to," said Janine. "But the Ice Devils have a playoff decider at the same time. They're my old team. Rowena's playing. Same thing. Do or die. I promised I'd be there to watch."

"Understood," said Sandy. "We're not really *your* team yet."

Janine could feel the frost in Sandy's voice. "Hey, that's not fair."

"Why not?" Sandy replied. "This team has let you and your friend come out, get in our way. Look, if we lose to Sherwood Park, your summer season is gonna be miserable, because I'm gonna be miserable. And I won't let you forget it."

You mean, you're not miserable right now? thought Janine. Then, out loud: "But the Ice Devils are my team."

Rowena broke in. "*Were* your team, Janine. *Were.*"

Playoffs

"What?" cried Janine. "Rowena?"

"Let's face it," Rowena said. "We aren't good this year. We're playing the South Side Angels. We've played them twice this year and didn't score a goal either time. The Ice Devils barely got into the playoffs. The Angels are in first place. Whether you're there or not, we're huge underdogs. You should be with your new team. You should be fitting in."

"Kid, you're not half bad," said Coach Laboucaine to Rowena as she walked into the lobby. "But your attitude sucks. Don't be so down on your team. Who cares if the Angels have beaten you twice? None of that matters on Saturday! Just like us. We've got a fresh slate when we play Sherwood Park!"

★ ★ ★

Janine and her father sat in the foyer of the Sherwood Park's Millennium Place arena. They looked through the large windows at the ice surface. Right away, Janine had been able to pick out The Chopper. She was clearly better than any of the other girls or boys on the Sherwood Park roster.

The Chopper scored the first goal of the game when she got to the front of the net and smashed a loose puck into the goal. Any time one of the Edmonton players got the puck, The Chopper descended on them as if she was a Star Wars TIE Fighter hunting X-Wings.

She was a predator — and the best player on the ice.

Janine's phone buzzed. She took her eyes off the game and looked at the screen. It was a message from Rowena.

End of 2nd. Down 3–1. Playing as well as we can. Will update.

OK, Janine texted back. GOOD LUCK!

"Who was that?" asked Janine's dad. He sat next to her, cradling a steaming mocha in his hand.

"Oh," said Janine. "Ice Devils down by two goals after two. Rowena says they are giving it their all."

"Look, it's tough for a team to bounce back when it loses its best player," said her dad. "I see that, even in the NHL. I know it's a team game. But when you lose your top player, it changes the way the whole team works together. I know you were disappointed when you watched the Ice Devils practice. But don't be too hard on them the next time you see them."

"They've still got a period to go," she said.

"That's true."

Janine looked up, brought back to the sledge hockey game by a piercing yell. It was so loud that it was easy to hear through the glass. It came from Sandy. The Chopper had smashed into her sled and the wreck took them both into the boards like stock cars into the wall.

Playoffs

PATIENT DIARY:

I haven't written in a while. But I feel a bit weird.
Rowena let me know that the Ice Devils' season
is over. They lost 5–3. I didn't see the game. And
it's weird that I don't feel as bothered about it as I
thought I'd be.

But what is really bugging me is Edmonton Athletics.
We lost 4–1 to Sherwood Park, and that Chopper
player Sandy talked about got a hat trick. Sandy got
injured and had to leave the game. I felt bad for Sandy,
even after I asked her if she was gonna be okay and
she told me to kiss her butt.

I've got to keep getting better so I can play real games
in time for the summer season.

Why does my old team losing in the playoffs not bug
me as much as the idea I might not make this team?

Weird.

16 THE PROJECT

Janine wheeled into class. Her parents were already there, sitting in chairs across from Mr. Massey's desk.

"Come in, Janine," said Mr. Massey. "It was great of your parents to come in during the day. I wanted us all to talk."

Janine wheeled into a spot between her mom and dad. "Am I in some sort of trouble?"

"Not at all," said Mr. Massey. He leaned back in his chair as far as it would go.

"The reason I called you in, Mr. and Mrs. Burnett, is obviously to talk about your daughter's work," he said. "Far too often, when I need to talk to parents, the principal is also present," he laughed. Mr. and Mrs. Burnett did not. "Okay, it's always a pleasure when I can speak to parents about how well their child is doing. And that's why I have you here."

"Okay, good. I was worried she was in trouble," Janine's mom said.

"I just wanted to tell you both — and Janine,

as well — that Janine's job-shadow report and her presentation to the class really struck a chord. Did she tell you about it?"

"I heard she gave you an alternate tour of the school," her dad said.

"Yes, and it was very powerful, really," said Mr. Massey. "I ended up talking to the other teachers about it. I talked to our principal about it. And not only is Janine getting an A for her work, I think it would be a shame if what she's done ends in our class."

"I showed the paper to my editor at the paper," said her dad. "He said he liked it. He told me it was interesting, but he couldn't possibly run it. He thought readers would take it the wrong way, and that could hurt the paper's connection with the team."

"I teach a little computer science," said Mr. Massey. "And I think Janine's paper, and her stories about how hard it is for her to access certain things, would make a great website. After Janine talked to the class, they really got behind her. They saw the world through her eyes. We could get a site, where Janine can share her stories, up and running quickly."

"That's a lot of work," said Janine.

"For sure, but I have a really great student who aces computer science. He could be a great help. I hope you don't mind, Janine, but I showed him your paper . . ."

"Stop!" Janine growled. *What made her snap at her teacher that way?*

"Janine," her mom cried. "What was that?"

"I know who he's talking about. Of course, Mr. Massey, you went and showed this to Marlon. The only other crippled kid in the school! So obvious!"

Mr. Massey got up from behind his desk. "Janine, I can see you are angry. But Marlon probably understands more than any of us what it's like to not be seen, just like you said in your presentation."

"Then get him to do this website by himself," Janine spat. And she turned and rolled out the door.

★ ★ ★

"You don't think you were a bit hard on your teacher?" asked Janine's dad, as he cut into his pork chop.

Janine took a gulp of water and looked at him across the dining room table.

"He's a dork," she said.

"You can't think that creating some website is a good idea, Jack," said Janine's mom. "We still need to present our statements on sentencing day. We can't have Janine talking about herself on a website anyone can access."

"Um, Trudy, that's not true," said Janine's dad. "She'd be writing about accessibility issues, which doesn't have anything to do with the crime itself. And she'd be hammering home the point of how difficult her life has become . . . "

The Project

Her dad stopped himself and looked at Janine. "I am so sorry."

"It's okay, Dad. No offence taken. Really, it's not a bad idea. I might have been interested. But that was before Mr. Massey went and searched out the only other crippled kid in school to help me."

"Can you not use the c-word?" her mom asked.

"Crippled. I am crippled, Mom. Marlon Williams is crippled. Crippled. Crippled. Crippled."

"Okay, Janine, take it down a notch," said her dad. "So, you would be interested, but the problem is Marlon. Correct?"

"Yes."

"And your issue with Marlon is . . .?"

"He said he was happy that I was in the accident."

"Oh," her dad set down his fork. "I see."

Her dad took another mouthful of food. He chewed for a very long time.

Then, he spoke again. "I understand that you might resent Marlon. It's clear that you two don't get along. Did you ever think about why he said that to you, or why you don't like him at all?"

"What do you mean, Dad?"

"I've worked with people in the past I didn't personally like. Editors. Copy editors. Other reporters. But we got along because we knew the work was more important than the personal differences we had. If Marlon is as good at designing websites as your teacher says, and you have passion for your writing, you could do some good things together."

"Ugh."

"Janine Burnett!" her dad said. *Wait, did he just raise his voice?* "Did you ever think that you don't like Marlon because you don't get the luxury of being the only kid in school who is disabled?"

"Jack!" Janine's mother scolded. "That's uncalled for!"

"That's not it!" Janine yelled, slamming her fork onto the table. "You can't read my mind! I wouldn't care if there were a hundred wheelchairs at my school! You want to know why I don't like Marlon? Because I don't remember him from before! When I was popular, he was the only kid who took the short bus to school and I didn't even know he existed. And, now, every day, he reminds me that I used to ignore him completely. Don't you see — I was just like the people I complain about now!"

Janine turned from the table. "You don't need to send me to my room. I'm already going."

"Wait, Janine." Her Dad put his hand up. "If you do decide to try putting together a website, think about what you just said to me. It might make for one heck of a blog post."

"What?"

"That kind of honesty? Readers will eat it up," he said. "And you should run the piece that my editor wouldn't consider. That also has a lot of passion and truth."

"Dad, I feel like you're railroading me. It's like you did with sledge hockey."

"Yeah, but you like sledge hockey, now."

Janine groaned and began to roll away.

"Don't leave the table," said her mom. "Finish your peas."

17 THE CHALLENGE

Coach Laboucaine stood at centre ice, a whistle hanging around her neck. The players formed a semicircle around her.

"I just wanted to say how much I appreciate all your efforts to make our club better." Her voice echoed through the arena. "While we didn't win a championship this year, both our senior and junior teams are looking forward to the summer season. And the prep for the summer season starts now. You have no idea how much I want us to improve this year. And how much I don't want Sherwood Park to win the summer championship!"

She cleared her throat as her players gave out a hearty set of *whoops* and *whoas*.

"Okay, everyone, calm down," she continued. "This summer, the junior team will have a new player. We are going to work Janine Burnett into our team. She's been working hard and, while she still needs work on a few things, I mean, *a lot* of things, she'll do a lot better by learning in game play. I've been impressed by her work ethic."

Rowena reached over to pat Janine on the back.

"Rowena, I see you. You are coming along, too — just not quite as quickly as Janine."

"Oh, I know," Rowena called back. "My arms burn after every practice."

"Don't think you're getting any sympathy from me, Cupcake," laughed the coach. "You've got to build up those dainty little arms of yours."

Janine looked over at Ryan. He took off his glove and gave her a thumbs-up. Then she looked over at Sandy. Sandy tried to look away, but Janine could feel her teammate's eyes burning through her.

★ ★ ★

The foyer was filled with the familiar smells the came from the arena's food stand — hot chocolate mixed with French fries. Sandy wheeled through the doors and parked right behind Janine.

"Joining the line for the bathroom?" said Janine.

"Yup," said Sandy. "This arena is accessible and the rink itself has big doors for the sleds. But the washroom space is still limited."

"At least it won't be used as a storeroom."

"Don't get your hopes up," Sandy said. "You're going to have to get used to this."

"Well, my teacher has convinced me to help put together a website about how difficult it is to get around. He wants me to help people see through the world through, well, our eyes."

"Really?" Sandy said.

"Sorry," Janine said. "I shouldn't have said anything. And I don't know why I'm telling you this. You hate me."

"You think I hate you?" Sandy shook her head.

"Of course. You smack into me every chance you get. You scowl at me every chance you get."

"Um, that's my game face," Sandy said. "On the ice, I take no prisoners. I take care of myself and my teammates. When you play against me, even in a scrimmage, you're in my crosshairs. Don't worry. When we start playing together in summer league, you'll see that I've got your back."

"But you also go on about how I'm a rookie and I think I'm special and . . ."

"Whoa," Sandy put her arms. "First off, damn straight I've been giving you hell. You need it. From the first practice, I could tell that you thought sledge hockey players were some kind of charity case. That's bull. And by now I think you know it. I've been crashing into you and been in your face to make you understand that I'm not here because I'm some charity case. I mean, geez, stop feeling sorry for yourself."

"So, you think me doing a website is another way for me to feel sorry for myself?"

Sandy laughed so hard she had to cover her mouth with her right hand. "Oh, wait. That's good. Like letting the world know about how hard it is to find an accessible bathroom is a way of feeling sorry for yourself? No! Damn straight we should let the world know how tough it can be."

"Oh."

"You should ask around about the crap we all have to put up with. Put that on your site."

"I didn't think we talked about that stuff . . ."

"Janine, we're teammates now. You'd be surprised what we talk about. We're not afraid to share. Take John Warnes. You know, Big Johnny on our team. He told me last week about how he got trapped when a construction crew closed the sidewalk in front of his family's condo. The only access they left was from the back stairs of his building. It did him no good, obviously. You should talk to him about that."

"Wow, I didn't know we were, that, well . . . open."

"If teammates aren't gonna look out for each other, who will? You think the notion of watching your teammate's back stops on the ice?"

"Well, there is one problem. I have to do this with another person at school and I'm not sure how to handle it. I think I was mean to him for a long time."

"You know what you should do? Invite him out for sledge hockey."

Janine thought it over. It wasn't a bad idea. And she could smash her sled into Marlon every once in awhile — all in the name of sharing and good fun.

18 A DIFFERENT KIND OF TEAMMATE

"Okay, Marlon, you're telling me we're about to go live."

"Yes," said Marlon. The blue glow of the computer screen was reflected in his glasses. "Unless you want to proofread your article again. I hear the nineteenth time is the charm."

"Wow, Marlon, I've learned something about you over these past couple of weeks," Janine said. She tried to peer over Marlon's shoulder.

"And that is?"

"You try to have a sense of humour. And you know what? It's actually . . ."

"Funny?"

"No, I wouldn't use that word. *Annoying*, maybe."

Marlon tapped the keys and the dashboard disappeared, replaced by a home page to Accessible.ca.

Access For Everyone, it said across the top, under the name.

Underneath that was a menu. Then, there were photos of Edmonton Athletics players on their sleds.

There was a spot to click on a video of the team's practice session and a link to the Canadian Paralympics site. There was a prompt asking readers to submit their photos and stories.

There was a *ping* on the site.

"What was that?" asked Janine.

"We already got a comment. On your story about covering the hockey game," said Marlon. "Maybe it's spam, maybe not."

Marlon hit a few more keys and rolled his finger across the track pad. He and Janine were alone in the darkened computer lab. They could hear the muffled sounds of students in the hallway, opening and closing locker doors, music and catcalls. All of the normal sounds of a junior high at lunchtime filtered in.

"It seems like a real comment. Already," Marlon whistled.

"Let me see!" said Janine.

YOU TOO CAN MAKE $1000 a DAY AT HOME!
FOLLOW THIS LINK FOR DETAILS! xxChanelGirl.ru

"Very funny," said Janine.

"It'll take a while for people to start noticing the site and for search engines pick it up," said Marlon. "But it's done. A couple of your articles, some photos of inaccessible spots that are supposed to be accessible."

"And now, you have to keep your part of the

deal. You have to come to the next open Edmonton Athletics practice," Janine said.

"Does this mean that we're, like, friends now?" said Marlon.

"Oh, no, it doesn't," Janine smiled. "Not at all. Marlon, you don't think I'm committing you to the worst workout of your life because I like you all of a sudden, do you? You're going to be paying a price. And I plan to collect."

Actually, Marlon isn't so bad, Janine thought to herself. *Sometimes, I guess you have to work with other people to make something happen. My dad and those other hockey writers aren't best friends, but they get along. They collect quotes for each other so all of them can get their assignments done. I don't have to be Marlon's best friend, either, but I don't have to be a total jerk around him. We can work together — and it's cool.*

The buzzer sounded that marked the end of lunch. Janine backed her wheelchair away from the desk.

"See you soon, Marlon," she said, coldly, like a threat, not a promise.

★ ★ ★

Janine drove one stick into the ice and then the other. The picks dug into the ice with each stroke, making her sled spring forward. She was a lioness on the savannah and poor Marlon was the gnu. His left arm pushed harder than the other, so his sled listed toward the boards on the right.

The puck was passed to Marlon. It bounced off the blade of his left stick, but stayed close enough that he could reach to retrieve it.

Janine was ten feet behind him.

Poor Marlon, Janine thought. *This is gonna be fun.*

Marlon lifted his head and slowed his sled. He frantically looked around for someone on his scrimmage team who was open for a pass. There were calls from other players, "I'm open!" "Here!" Another player banged his stick on the ice, asking for the puck.

But Marlon couldn't see or hear them. He knew Janine was coming at him from behind.

She was now less than seven feet from her quarry.

I'm coming, she thought.

Panicked, Marlon tried to slap the puck away. Whether by design or blind luck, he hit it just right. The puck found a gap between the other team's defenders. It hit the goalie's sled and ricocheted off the tubes and blades. The puck crossed the goal line.

There was a roar from Marlon's teammates. Sandy started to scream, "Beginner's luck!" But she was interrupted by the crunch of metal on metal.

Marlon's sled scooted sideways into the wall.

"Lucky goal, Marlon!" Janine cried. She was satisfied that her target had been neutralized. "Luck-eeeeee! But that was for being happy I'm in the van with you! Oh boy! Now we're even!"

"Coach," Sandy called out. "You know what? I think we might finally have a player on our team as mean as The Chopper."

Ryan called to Janine. "The ice in your blood runs cold. Geez, I remember our first practice. You didn't even know how to keep your sled straight! Now you're a killer out there! An assassin!"

19 COMING TO TERMS

Marlon and Janine waited by the arena doors. Her dad had texted to warn them that he was going to be a little late picking them up.

Marlon had his tablet in his hands.

"Well, our Alexa ranking is like, up over two millionth in the world."

"So, we've got what? Five visitors? All people who know us?" said Janine. "I guess no one really cares about *Access For Everyone*."

"No, no!" Marlon smiled. "Do you have any idea how many websites there are in the world? This ranking is actually pretty good! We're getting well over a thousand visitors a day. That's really solid for a new website that doesn't advertise."

"I've picked up another hundred Twitter followers," said Janine. "So, it might explain that."

"And we're getting comments!" Marlon said. He swiped his fingers across the tablet screen. "Wait, whoa."

Coming to Terms

"Marlon, you're not going to fool me with the spam trick again."

"No, check this out! It was posted as a comment and a message to the site!"

Dear Janine,

On behalf of Edmonton's pro hockey club and the league, we'd like to thank you for the story you told. We make our best efforts to make our games accessible to all — our fans, our employees and those who work covering the team.

But you brought to light some areas we can improve upon. We have raised them with League headquarters in New York, and the League is supportive.

On behalf of the club, we want to invite your Edmonton Athletics team to play and/or practise on our arena's ice. We would like you to come before or after one of our team's practices, so our players can watch and be inspired by the work you and your teammates put in. Our ice surface is accessible and your dressing rooms will be, as well.

Please contact our club and we can plan a time early in the new season to make this happen!

Yours thankfully,
Walter Day
Director of Communications
Edmonton Professional Hockey Corp.

Sandy wheeled out of the dressing room and into the foyer.

"Sandy, you've got to see this!" Janine cried out. Marlon handed the tablet to Janine, who handed it to Sandy.

"Wow, you've got them paying attention!" said Sandy. "This is almost as good as it would be to beat Sherwood Park!"

★ ★ ★

Janine sat in front of the laptop in her room. The Crown Prosecutor had just emailed back to her the umpteenth draft of her victim-impact statement. There were more suggested edits. Could she write more about what it was like in the hospital? Had she lost any friends at school? How did her parents have to remodel the house?

Janine closed her eyes and tried to remember the accident. It was still a blank in her memory. *She is looking at the trophy that is next to her on the back seat. She is thinking about the winning goal. And then she wakes up in a hospital bed with more tubes coming out of her than Frankenstein's monster.*

She'd never met James Colangelo, the driver of the other car. She only knew about him through the newspaper reports. But the Crown Prosecutor had told Janine that Colangelo had done the right thing by agreeing to plead guilty and avoid a long court case. Janine and her parents wouldn't need to testify in court.

So, why do I still need to write this stupid statement? thought Janine. *The lawyers say they'll agree to a sentence, then present it to the judge for me to approve. What difference does this statement make now?*

Janine's mom walked into the room. "I was just coming to remind you that you need to get that new draft of the statement in. But I see you're already working on it! You want me to read it?"

"No, I'm fine," Janine said.

Janine waited for her mom to leave the room. She waited to hear the reassuring click of her bedroom door closing. Then, she started scrolling through the draft.

My name is Janine Burnett. To the court: I thought I'd let you about how my life has changed . . .

Blah, blah, blah, Janine thought. *All I'm doing is writing exactly what the lawyers and my mom want me to write.*

Janine chose the menu item to "select all" and hit the Delete button. Instead of a statement, she was now looking at a blank white page on her screen. She smiled and began to type.

Nothing I write today is going to change what happens. Mr. Colangelo is going to get a three-month sentence, and he'll likely be out earlier than that. He's not a criminal, after all. He's just a bad driver who made a really bad error in judgment.

In her head, Janine heard her mother hissing her name. She ignored it.

I was going to tell you that Mr. Colangelo had given me a life sentence. Then I thought about it. If I say it, do I believe it myself? Do I believe that the rest of my life is, well, a life sentence? If I do, what do I have to live for?

I don't want to see my life as a sentence. I think my mom does, and I'm sad about that. It's not the life I had imagined for myself. But it might give me the chance to make a difference. I can make people aware of the challenges I face. I can start us talking about how we can make things more accessible. I can still play sports and dream of one day being good enough to play for Canada, even though I am still a long way off.

Then I thought, if I write about how sorry for myself I am, I'm just spreading the idea that being in a wheelchair is something to be pitied. My best friend has been saying for a long time that my pity party has to stop. She's right. I don't want to give people the idea that my life is less worthwhile. So instead of saying how bad I feel, I want the court to pass on these three words to Mr. Colangelo:

I forgive you.

Coming to Terms

Janine looked across the table at her mother. The light from the phone cast an eerie bluish glow on Mrs. Burnett's face.

She's reading the statement, I just know it, Janine thought.

Her mom turned off her phone. She looked directly at Janine.

"Janine Burnett."

"Yes?" Janine thought. *Oh no, she's gonna blow.*

"Janine Anna Burnett."

Oh, wow, she's using my middle name. That means I am in a lot of trouble.

A tear rolled slowly down her mother's cheek. "Janine, I need to tell you something."

"What? How disappointed you are in me?"

"No, not at all. Your statement has made me see something. I'm proud of you. And if this is what you want to tell the world, I need to stop controlling you. You understand? I've been grieving for you since I woke up in the hospital. I haven't let the anger go. And I realize that we need to move on, that I need to move on."

20 A BIG HIT

Coach Laboucaine talked to her players as they got into their sleds.

"Okay, first game of the summer season. Let's knock the smiles off those Sherwood Park faces! Joe, make sure they don't win the battles in front of our net. Sandy, I need you to focus on getting to the net. Ryan, they are quick near the boards, so, cut off the middle. And Janine, yes, Janine. Just, well, have fun — and stay alive!"

Janine and her teammates slid out to the centre of the ice. The Sherwood Park team took their positions on the other side of the red line.

Ryan tapped Janine on the shoulder. "You'll do fine," he said as he swooped past.

The Chopper wore a black helmet. It was like all the other black helmets. But right on the top of the helmet was a sticker of a skull and crossbones.

"Hey, newbie!" she called out, pointing one of her sticks directly at Janine. "I can't wait to get to know you a little better!"

A Big Hit

"Just play the game," Sandy barked.

The puck dropped and the sleds crashed as if they were boats swept away by a tsunami. The puck went out toward the boards, with Sandy in hot pursuit. Janine, knowing Sandy was going to get the puck, cut to the middle of the ice. She drove forward on her sticks as fast as she could.

Janine's arms didn't burn as badly as they had after her first few practices. But she could still feel the strain in her forearms and shoulders.

Sandy got the puck and slipped a short pass to Ryan, who was cutting ahead of her on the wing. A Sherwood Park sled descended on him right away, a stick ready to knock the puck away. Ryan flipped the puck to the middle of the ice, near the blue line. It bounced off the tube of a Sherwood Park player's sled and into Janine's range.

Janine planted her left stick mightily into the ice. She swerved the sled and reached out with her right stick. The puck on her stick, there was still a defender and a goalie to beat. But Janine knew she didn't have to beat them alone. Sandy would be hot on her tail. If Janine could bring the defender to her, she could slip the puck into her teammate's path for a shot on goal.

Of course, the player rushing at Janine was none other than The Chopper. *She is so quick*, Janine thought, feeling like a sitting duck on the ice. *Sandy, where are you?*

Stick Pick

Out of the corner of Janine's eye and through her face guard, Sandy's bright red helmet popped into view.

Janine moved forward, looking to meet The Chopper head on. It was like a game of chicken on the ice. The Chopper came hard, clearly not looking to back out of the impending collision. Just before impact, Janine sent the puck in Sandy's direction. Janine never saw if the puck reached its intended target. She was spinning and sliding backward at the same time. Her head snapped back from the force of the collision.

As her sled came to rest, she tried to see what had happened. Then she saw Sandy sliding toward her. Sandy was smiling.

"Not bad for your first real shift!" Sandy said. "Your first assist!"

★ ★ ★

Sherwood Park was putting on the pressure — Edmonton Athletics was holding on. What had been a 2–0 lead for Edmonton evaporated. Sherwood Park scored two quick goals early in the third period to tie the game.

The next goal would likely be the winner. Janine was the last player back as Sherwood Park came at Edmonton on a two-on-one break. The puck carrier decided to throw the puck toward the net. Her Sherwood Park teammate — The Chopper — brought her sled toward the net as fast as she could.

A Big Hit

Janine could let the puck go past her and avoid a collision with the player bearing down on her. Or she could try to get the puck out of danger. There really was no decision. The game was tied. She had to do everything she could to break up the scoring chance.

Janine drove the picked end of her right stick into the ice, bracing for impact. With her left stick, she swatted at the puck as The Chopper bore down on her. Janine got the puck away from the goal, but the sledges made a banging noise that echoed through the arena.

The jagged end of The Chopper's stick dug into Janine's left forearm. Two sledges, two players, locked together by The Chopper's stick, embedded in Janine's arm. They finally came to a standstill when they hit the end boards.

When the Coach Laboucaine got to the mess, Janine had one thing to say. The best she could muster was a whisper.

"Did they score?"

The coach shook her head. "You did good."

★ ★ ★

"Hi, I'm Doctor Finn." He was tall and wore a long white coat that sort of whooshed behind him. He pulled the curtains apart to enter and then back together behind him.

Janine sat in a chair next to the gurney. Caked, blackened blood covered her left arm. Janine's mom sat at the end of the bed. Her eyes were red as she tried to dry tears from her cheeks with a tissue.

There was a machine next to Janine that had a flashing heart symbol. The display read "Pulse: 86." There was a red monitor clipped to her finger, with a wire that led to another machine. That one showed "Oxygen: 95%."

"So, what do we have here?" asked the doctor.

"Hockey," Janine hissed through her busted lip.

The doctor shone a light into Janine's eyes. He held up a finger and waved it in front of her face. "Can you follow my finger with your eyes?"

"Yes, I can," Janine mumbled. "Am I okay, doctor?"

Janine's mother broke in. "She got into a collision — actually many — in her hockey game. Her sled met the other one head-on. High speed."

"Don't they have helmets and masks?" asked the doctor.

"Yes," said Janine. "Mine came off in the collision."

The doctor examined Janine's bloodied arm.

Janine's mom turned to her. "Why did you do such a stupid thing? Look how badly you're hurt!"

"This is going to need stitches," said the doctor, looking at the gash on the arm. "And we'll get you something for the pain right away. You did this playing sledge hockey? Wait, Miss, are you smiling?"

"Yes," Janine said through clenched teeth.

How could she explain it to the doctor and her mom? Throwing herself in harm's way to stop a scoring chance had made her feel alive. Her heart was pumping. She couldn't wait to get back on the ice.

"I hope this leaves a pretty good scar," she said.

"What?" said the doctor.

"What?" her mom coughed.

"When I get back on the ice, I'm gonna look so tough," Janine said, still smiling. "Battle scars."

ACKNOWLEDGEMENTS

This book is the product of both my imagination and quite a bit of research. I'd like to thank the following people for their advice, wisdom and support:

Dean Krawec, team manager for Alberta Sledge, for helping me with the ins and outs of what a beginner will face in sledge hockey;

Ing Wong-Ward, the associate director, Centre for Independent Living in Toronto, for her insight;

And my brother Charles, for helping me understand the post-accident process, from disbelief to grief to acceptance.

It is my hope that Janine felt as real to you as she did to me.

MARQUIS

Québec, Canada